ARE YOU HUNGRY
ARE YOU COLD

ARE YOU HUNGRY
ARE YOU COLD

by LUDWIG BEMELMANS

THE WORLD PUBLISHING COMPANY

CLEVELAND AND NEW YORK

Published by The World Publishing Company
2231 West 110th Street, Cleveland 2, Ohio

Published simultaneously in Canada by
Nelson, Foster & Scott Ltd.

Library of Congress Catalog Card Number: 60-11452

FIRST EDITION

With the exception of Hitler,
who really was a dog,
it must be stated that the
persons and places in this story
are other than here put down.

CONTENTS

PART ONE

CONTENTS

PART ONE

1. LIGHT CAVALRY

WHEN WE WERE very little, I and my brother Hugo, who was a year older, loved our rabbits, turtle, and toys. We adored the Christ child and the crèche in which he lay, the donkeys and cows that stood in that crèche, and the live ones in the fields about the place where we lived. We said our prayers and included Mama and Papa in them. Of them we knew little for we were in the hands of two nursemaids the day long.

Although dressed in the proper fashion as such, our nurses were peasant girls from the neighborhood, and roughly courted by the entire regiment. We therefore were always near the stables and places where the soldiers were sitting around. They lay around on the grass or on the benches, wherever our nurses were, and they kissed them— and us—and always had their hands on some part of the nurses.

The names of our nurses were Sophie and Caroline. Both of them had round faces, beautiful clear complexions, and they were so healthy that their cheeks were as if painted.

They liked to walk barefoot and they laughed easily. They had endless patience, loved us as if we were their own children, and allowed us to do whatever we wanted. They were also gay with the soldiers, and the soldiers played with us, throwing us in the air and catching us, playing hide-and-seek; and the soldiers played also with the nurses, sometimes so roughly that they were pushed away, not angrily, but with shrieks of laughter.

The soldiers were very nice to us, and they talked very freely in the slang of the region, and when we repeated some of the words they said, and the names they called Papa, they roared with laughter and brought us candy, or led us about on the smaller horses. The nurses giggled, and it was a very free early childhood. We were not burdened with anything in the way of discipline except the rudimentary business of becoming housebroken; we lived like young dogs those first years around the stables.

The soldiers threw us from one to the other and into the hay, and played games with us. And there were always new ones when the others were tired. We listened to them practice fanfares with the beautiful beflagged trumpets that are twisted and blown like angry cocks crowing.

It smelled of horses and leather. We were lifted up and allowed to bang on the mounted kettledrums, we watched the animals being groomed, and everywhere there were things of interest.

The soldiers received packages from home and there was always candy or a chocolate cake, a slice of sausage or a bit of ham. We were always hungry and the milk came directly from the cows, warm and foaming. Every evening we came back streaked and incredibly dirty, and we were taken in the servants' entrance and up the backstairs.

And there in our rooms we were put into the tub from which we emerged neat and clean and fit for inspection in the military establishment that was our home. It was evening then and all the loudness and activity in the fields and the stables magically came to a halt. The last trumpet sounded and Papa shouted his last command and the world of Beaufort came to a magnificent parade halt, only to be awakened and examined the next morning and again inspected and shouted at by Papa.

I think of it always in the early morning with dew, frost, or snow on the ground, gilded by the rising sun, with puffed birds sitting on branches as if wearing brown and gray sweaters, with golden trumpets playing and shouts of command and the sound of drums. The road that was always marked with horse-hoof imprints, the blue-gray water from which vapors rose—and veils of which slowly moved over the parade grounds and shooting ranges that lay between the hills and forests. In all this was a loud immense red patch, violent in color, like tomato juice, and with a blue roof and towers of gray stone—the castle from which we came early in the morning, bundled up, sometimes carried half the way and sometimes running. Then it seemed an immense distance, for our legs were very small.

We came out the backdoor of the house, passed the gray covered garbage cans that stood like soldiers in a straight line on a wooden platform, crossed a small courtyard, and went through a formal garden with trees so clipped that they looked like short-legged policemen in capes, drawn up for review on both sides of the path. Then we went through a fruit-and-vegetable garden with rows of cabbages, carrots, Brussels sprouts on long stems, with espalier fruit growing on walls, with cherry, apple, and plum trees, walked on a path lined with black currant bushes, and finally, passing a hothouse, we came to a gate. And there the true paradise began.

Somebody always shouted our names in greeting—sometimes one soldier, sometimes a group of soldiers. The horses were neighing: it smelled of animals and the stables. Dogs, lambs, and goats came toward us, pigs grunted, and the rooster on the biggest dung heap in France stopped scratching, shook his magnificent plumage, and said something in his garrulous cockerel language before strutting off again to his business of eating, scratching, and making love.

The animals all made love; they kissed each other, licked each other's faces, and then wiggle-waggled together for awhile, and after this the mother animals got fatter, and then there were young ones and we needed no dolls or toys, for we were always supplied with baby rabbits, donkeys, or lambs, and we watched the first efforts at standing up of calves, and of foals, and helped them drink from their mothers.

Sometimes we were allowed up late when a new one was born. We saw the cow with her rasping tongue cleaning off her baby, and we looked on with wonder when a little chicken, duck, or gosling broke out of its shell and immediately knew what he was and how to run, swim, and eat and how to hide under the mother's wings when danger threatened.

Between the castle and the stables was the chapel, where the good Father Martinez, a small old gentleman, rendered glory to God without end. When I think of the Lord in Heaven there appears before me clearly this saintly man in his black, patched soutane that shone like mother-ofpearl, and in his heavy-soled boots that were like boats. He was the kindest soul I have met in my life.

In his little church the soldiers were silent, shy, and ashamed as they approached the confessional where he listened to them, and gave them his benediction, mild reproach, or advice and the lightest penitence possible.

We wanted very much to confess to him but it was denied us, for we were too young, and in his eyes evidently incapable of sin. We prayed, however, with our hands pressed together, like the wooden angels at the side of the altar, and intently and with closed eyes, for whatever animals were ill, for Sophie and Caroline, and for Papa and Mama and for ourselves.

The person who ranked highest in Beaufort, the one regarded by all with a mixture of respect and admiration, was mostly seen upon his fine horse. Always immaculate, and straight and very beautiful, he was our father who was in command of the cavalry school. The nurses had so much respect for him that they carefully timed our exits and entrances to the castle in which we lived so as not to risk a meeting. Our nursery was away from the living quarters of our parents and we could make as much noise as we wanted, and, in general, it was as if we were the offspring of animals that let their young run from them as soon as they had the use of their legs.

It was in late autumn, the cauliflower had been almost all harvested, but there were cabbage and cauliflower leaves about and I picked these up to give to the rabbits of which there were more and more and who ate more and more continuously. I was busy with this, when I saw my father arrive on foot. He always carried a stick or a riding crop under his arm. The stick he carried that day was very beautifully worked with a silver tip and handle and a band with a crest on it. I ran toward him; I was bundled in an old sweater and several shawls and had my leaves in a basket. I said something, and he stopped and looked at me from head to foot. Then he put the silver tip of his stick on my sweater, on my chest, and slowly pushed me, so that I stood in the opposite direction from which the wind came. The nurse came running, my father touched her with his stick to keep her at distance, and with nostrils distended he said that I smelled most awfully, and he told her that it was disgusting to have a child in such a state— inadmissible. He yelled, "Go and go quickly, and clean her up and yourself as well." Sophie stammered, and picked me up, and Papa turned abruptly and marched off into the castle.

Our mother was equally remote from us. We saw our parents on the rarest occasions, after long scrubbing and brushing and being dressed. We saw them toward evening when we were ready for bed, and were taken down the wide stairway in nightshirts, slippers, and robes, and there at the bottom of the stairs we were sometimes presented to visitors or relatives but always quickly dismissed and sent back.

2. THE EVENING BELLS

AMONG THE SOLDIERS was one who was very big and powerful, but of a quiet nature. Handsome, and with a mustache,
he was honored for he was the pivot man at drills, and
Papa, who prized the proper appearance of his regiment
above everything, was considering him for drum major
or some function in which the big bearlike man could be
dressed and behung with glitter so that he would be the
emblem of all things gloriously military. He had had some
training but it was difficult work, for while he played
proudly on his kettledrums, he was not a parade soldier.
He was a shy, kindly man, and he sat in corners polishing
his drums or his leather fittings and singing quietly to himself. He rested his big blue eyes on Sophie and they sat
sometimes for long periods hand in hand or walked that
way. He lifted both of us and carried us in his arms, and
let us climb all over him. He talked, as all other soldiers
did, the slang of the region.

They called him Hercule, on account of his strength,
and they called Papa the Lion of Beaufort and other names,

which, when we repeated them, made them roar with laughter. Hercule let us ride on his horse, one in back, one in front of him. It spread our legs wide, for he had the biggest horse, the one that also carried the kettle-drums when the grand parades took place. When Hercule rode with the drums and beat them, everybody watched him with pride. He did not dare look at us when he passed by, but smiled straight ahead to let us see that he knew we were there, and he gave his bamboo hammers, which had round leather-covered pads like snowballs at the ends, an extra swing so that the kettledrums resounded like shots.

Toward evening, when it was time to go back to the castle, the bells of the church rang, and the steeple was so close that the sound of the bells touched us, like the wings of a bird flying past. Hugo and I were busy rounding up our rabbits, and one night one of them had hopped away and into the stable where the hay for the horses was kept. His white tail bobbed up and down like a little lamp and we followed him. Inside the stable we lost him, but after awhile we saw, in front of us, Sophie and Hercule. They were kissing, and he leaned over her as she lay in the still green grass hay—a bed of clover and flowers. And now he was on his elbows, and again he kissed her, and then she raised her skirt—she wore nothing under it— and her strong limbs were like wax and honey in color and the round knees turned upward. Hercule was busy with his trousers, he sank to his knees, and then there was a small sound from Sophie, half pain, half pleasure, and then they wiggle-waggled the way the animals did—with the one difference that they were face to face and could kiss each other—and it lasted awhile and when it was over, Hercule kissed Sophie, she straightened out her hair, and then her dress, he helped her up, and they passed us and went out into the yard.

After they were gone, Hugo let himself fall over backward and he said, "Is it possible? Did you see?"

I said, "Yes, I saw—"

"Then Mama and Papa do the same thing—"

"Yes—"

"—and that is why we are here, like the rabbits and the lambs and horses."

This tremendous discovery held us spellbound, and filled us with great warmth and security. It gave us a place in our paradise with all that lived. We went out to where Sophie and Hercule stood hand in hand, and Hercule picked us both up and carried us to the castle, and we watched Sophie as she put us to bed and we wondered when she would have her baby. It seemed to go very slowly.

Now we also included in our prayers the one who would be born, and all things took on new meaning and importance. We did not speak to Sophie about what we knew, but it spoke to us through her, for she changed. She was not as we expected; for awhile she looked empty rather than full, like a hollow tree, and so did Hercule, and they walked about hand in hand, but sadly and by themselves on remote paths, earnestly talking, and then when she began to get a large stomach and walked and sat differently than she had before, she wept. Then we told her that we knew she would have a baby and she held us close and wept some more and we said that she should be happy.

She shook her head and cried and trembled, and we asked her why and she said because she and Hercule were not man and wife. So we asked her why not, and she said that Hercule had to ask our father's permission to marry. When we asked why he didn't she said because Hercule was afraid, and because he should have asked long ago and now it was too late, and that we could not possibly understand how terrible it was. So we asked if Hercule had asked the good Father Martinez what to do. She said that they had both confessed to Father Martinez, and that he had told them to go to Papa and ask him for permission to marry. Then why didn't they? Because Papa was a very severe man. So time went on, and we were as sad as Hercule and Sophie, and we thought of going to Papa ourselves, but then we didn't know him very well, and we also understood why Hercule did not go. Why didn't the good Father Martinez go? He had offered, but they had begged him not to and Hercule had promised he would— he always said he would the next day, or next week.

It was convenient that it was autumn again, for Sophie had good reason to put on sweaters and coats to hide her condition, and now more than ever we were careful not to encounter Papa anywhere.

All the people in the castle knew about it, although it was a secret as far as Papa was concerned, and a whisper hung all about the big place. Hercule polished his drums and cleaned his horse. Otherwise he made himself scarce: he seemed not to be here. Father Martinez blessed the hounds for the hunt, pheasants and boar were shot. There were golden or dark red leaves on branches here and there, the fog thickened on the fields, and vapors rose from the nostrils of the horses and animals and from our own noses and mouths. Poor Sophie cried and lay on her bed and the midwife said that soon the baby would be born.

The big strong Hercule still polished his kettledrums

that were now like the big round stomach of poor Sophie and he still promised to see Papa next week—and then it happened, with the help of everyone.

It happened late after the evening bells and after the good Father Martinez had married them without Papa's permission. It was almost Christmas, then, and Father Martinez had his hands full. He sprinkled some water on the head of the little boy and gave them both a small gift. It was one of the miracles that he, who never had anything for himself, always had something for others. He got Sophie the things she needed, the baby stayed in the village, and Hercule looked a little happier, although it was still a secret. Nobody mentioned the baby in the castle and we made ourselves small when we came home and ran upstairs quickly. And then it was Christmas.

Father Martinez worked always, everywhere, and now there were more things to do than usual, for he prepared the Christmas crèche. The soldiers helped him and brought pine trees and swept the barn, and they built and hammered and Father Martinez was busy with electric wires and colored lights, and finally it was all finished.

A golden star hung from the ceiling, and the people who were in the nativity play came, and to show the world of Beaufort that the newborn was a most important person, the baby of Hercule and Sophie was put in swaddling clothes and into the cradle, where he lay smiling, and making his punching and kicking movements and looking all around him at the many lights. To his right were the animals whose soft eyes were as if filled with tears. Then the large doors of the barn creaked on their hinges and opened and in came the Wise Men. They were tall Senegalese from a regiment of Spahis, dressed in long blue capes. They had gotten off their caparisoned white horses, and with majesty they walked into the barn, moving slowly, and placing their gifts before the Christ child.

The music of the regiment played and above all, loud and rolling, were the drums of Hercule. We stood with Sophie, who had let go of our hands to dry her tears, but now she was happy and lifted us up and kissed us. The people who crowded the barn made room, and Mama, Papa, and the officers and their ladies appeared, and gazed at the crèche with solemn expressions and then they went to Midnight Mass. The band moved over into the church and carried their instruments up into the choir.

After the music had started, we were taken back by Sophie and Caroline. The bells of the church rang out, the night was blue like the roof of the castle. We walked back in the cracking snow and thanked God in our beds that all in his world was so beautiful.

3. PAPA AND THE GREAT SOCIETY
OF TIN SOLDIERS

MY BROTHER HUGO was never allowed to play with tin soldiers, for they all belonged to Papa, like the live ones. If he had had his own tin soldiers, he would have been immediately suspected of having taken them from Papa's collection.

We had not seen any of them, but the soldier who ran between the stables and the castle, and Auguste, the deaf chauffeur, had told us about them. A whole large room was given over to the collection. Whereas other people had a billiard table, Papa had an immense table with a strong light over it, and along the walls there were specially made closets with felt-lined drawers, and in these were all the regiments of the French army, mostly during Napoleon's time, with all the material a moving army needs: with forage wagons, caissons, military trains, field hospitals, pontoon bridges, and the thousand and one items in the inventory of soldiering. The figures had always to be put away neatly in their drawers by Auguste and the soldier who was called the Killer.

They also had to put away the "Kriegspiel," a game so called because it was playing at war.

It consisted of countless maps, also in special drawers, and a pincushion the size of a footstool, stuck into which were pins of all sizes and colors, representing friend and enemy: army corps, battalions, companies, individual batteries, soldiers, generals, all that makes up an army. These pins were stuck into the map according to the way the troops were on the field at the beginning of the battle to be refought, and then the progress of the battle was shown, as it was, or as it might have been if either side had done something other than it had actually done, or if, for example in the case of the battle of Waterloo, it had not rained, and so Napoleon had won. This game lasted late into the night, and usually was played between two officers, usually of equal rank. Papa played with other colonels.

There was another more solitary game, and that was the making of small dioramas. This was a great hobby and took much patience. First a box was made, of a size to accommodate the scene. Then the background was painted in and scenery built—houses, trees, rocks—and then it would be a reproduction of a large battle which had taken months; or just a small scene, like a house burning and a woman running from it with a baby in her arms, and in front, three unsaddled horses and three hussars, talking together, or a corner of a field, with Napoleon, his spyglass fully extended and resting on the shoulder of a grenadier, watching a battle.

What was most important was that all the details of uniform, equipment, and arrangement were exact. There were collectors who showed these works of art, others who kept them for themselves and a few intimate friends. Papa was one of those who kept his collection to himself and he did not like anyone to see it, except a brother colonel who could appreciate it. He had made many of these small theaters of war.

The soldiers were designed in France, and then the designs were sent to Nuremberg, Germany, where the molds were made. Then the soldiers were sent back to France, where artists carefully colored them. It was a very costly hobby, and a collection of the soldiers was very valuable and had to be treated with great care.

There were other soldiers also, not flat like the tin ones, but round and very beautiful and made of lead. Each of these soldiers had his little place to go back to, in a drawer also lined with felt. It took hours to do all this putting away and the Killer was excused from all other duty. Next to the regiment, the leaden and tin soldiers were the most important item in Papa's life, and on account of this and because he was always around Papa, the Killer enjoyed a very special position, even though he had no rank.

He was often promoted but always broken again because he was a gypsy. He came from a circus and could stand upside down, with his hand on top of the head of another soldier. He could throw knives and juggle, ride standing on a horse, pick things from the floor while galloping, knew wonderful stories, knew how to cook, blow smoke rings, imitate animals so they would think he was one of them, and talk to them as well. He was also a parachutist and had been in Africa and everywhere else. He could jump from a plane and we had seen him do it, close to the ground. He never answered a question we asked with an "I don't know," but talked to us as if we were grown-up people and deserved a serious answer. Because he was always around Papa he was always meticulously dressed and walked and talked like Papa. He served at table in the house. He was very good-looking, all sinews, muscles, veins, and bones. He boxed, wrestled, sang, played the guitar—there was nothing he could not do, including climbing the outside of the castle from the ground to the roof. With all this he could have been a general, we believed, but whenever he was promoted, he did something and slipped back again. He shared with our father a great love of horses and uniforms and tin soldiers, and he was unhappy about the army becoming mechanized and very proud that Papa fought for retaining all possible trappings and glory, if for nothing else than for just a parade now and then, and the pleasure of inspecting it and seeing it pass in review. When Papa inspected the troops in their parade best, he always stopped, put his stick under his arm, and called the regimental sergeant and tailor to adjust the fit of a jacket, to correct this or that, and he saw at once every fault, every button not buttoned. He spent a great deal of time on Hercule, who was a special problem as he tended to stoop instead of making the best of his powerful chest.

The Killer drove a jeep to which he had attached at the front an iron grille with large iron spikes like the points of lances, inclined slightly upward, and also like meat hooks, and with this car he drove into the forests at night at great speed, with all the headlights on brightly, and he came back with deer, hare, wild pigs, pheasants, and other animals which he hunted this way.

This was not altogether to our liking, but he explained that in winter especially the animals, who had many enemies besides man, often died in terrible agony, and that this was a quick and merciful end and that they ran by themselves into his machine and would have been run over had it been another vehicle. Now, he said, they were sleeping peacefully, and when we patted their fur and feathers we persuaded ourselves that it was agreeable to be sleeping like that, never to have to look for food again, or fear the cold or old age or a slow painful end. We agreed to think this way mainly because we wanted to like the Killer, and also it was easier because these animals were not our own and we did not know them.

Whatever knowledge we had of Papa we got from the Killer. He told us about Papa's bath.

Papa got up at six o'clock. First a large, floating thermometer had to be put into the water and the temperature had to be exactly 104 degrees. Bath salts of lavender scent were put in the water. There were two large flacons of Eau de Cologne, also lavender-scented. Those were for the rubdown after the bath. In winter the bathrobe and towels had to be warmed. Twice a week a complete set of manicure instruments had to be laid out, for he did his nails himself, and there were things to stop the bleeding if he cut himself doing his nails or shaving. For shaving he used a sharp, minuscule instrument, in the design of a small saber, which he had gotten from Spain. After his bath, he took a cold shower, then the rubdown, then the shave, then twice a week the manicure. He had a closet of pills, in all colors, and he took his medicines next. He did not allow anybody to see him in his bath, but the maid once asked the Killer: "What is the Colonel doing while he is in his tub?" for there were noises as long as he was in it. Eventually it was found out that Papa had a theory that it was very bad to lie still in the bathtub, and he did exercises in the water which sounded as if a seal was taking a bath. The most important room was next to his bath, and here in closets hung all his uniforms, boots, caps, hats, and civilian and golf clothes. There stood also a wooden horse on which Papa sat when his tailor made him new riding clothes. On a table with a white towel were a dozen cream-colored gloves, laid in a row, and his handkerchiefs which the Killer had to atomize with lavender. There was a humidor for his cigarettes, which were scented with a perfume called Mitsuko. There was also a rack for sabers and a place for guns, and his famous sticks, of which he had a great collection, as well as riding crops in all lengths, and last a glass case in which his various ribbons and medals were kept.

After Papa was dressed, which took an hour, he went back into his bedroom, opened the window, and took deep breaths, always three of them, inhaling "ahhhhhhh" and exhaling "fhssssssss"—three; not two, not four, always three. Auguste, the chauffeur who was deaf, waited below for the appearance of Papa to breathe. That gave him time to get the car ready, for it was forty-five minutes from then that Papa appeared at the door of the castle. Meantime, he came downstairs, and Mama had come downstairs from her apartment, and they had breakfast together. He kissed her on the forehead, and then sat down opposite her and always at the exact time he got up, kissed her hand, and left.

Then came the car with Auguste. This soldier had been with Papa in the last war. There was between them a kind of friendship, a liaison that officers permit themselves oc-casionally with good soldiers. This one had the rank of sergeant. He had been taught lip reading and when he looked at my father he understood his orders. When he drove and his back was turned, if Papa wanted to change direction he had a set of signals for Auguste to tell him which way he wanted to go. He tapped him with the stick on the right or left shoulder.

Auguste had a habit of saying in answer to all orders, "D'accord, mon Colonel," and this seemed overly familiar to Papa, who did not want agreement but demanded absolute obedience. One day, when he had had enough of this, he said: "Auguste, if you say once more 'd'accord mon Colonel' I will have you thrown into solitary." To which Auguste, with his hands on the seams of his trousers, replied: "D'accord, mon Colonel." This did not amuse Papa, for he had no sense of humor, and as the chauffeur turned he gave him a kick in the backside with his boot. He did this only because Auguste had been with him for many years and was like a member of the family. Otherwise, although a strict disciplinarian, Papa was always correct and never allowed himself or anyone else to hit even the rawest recruit. He did it all with words and in this he was master. That time, with the boot, Auguste lowered his head and said: "Merci, mon Colonel" in the tradition of thanking for punishment. Papa gave up trying to change the phrase "D'accord, mon Colonel" but it was the only instance in which he gave up. When the Killer told us these stories of home, which he often did with the soldiers sitting around listening and laughing and making remarks, we always asked to be told again and again. And, ever since we had made the great discovery in the stable, we also wondered where and when and how we had been made.

Now the Killer sat with Hercule, who was busy with

his big hands polishing leather and cleaning his horse, for there was a parade rehearsal with music and the Killer said that he should tell Papa about his wife and baby. "Everyone else knows," said the Killer, "the top sergeant, the village, and most probably the Colonel also knows and just wants to be told." On the parade ground, the Colonel would surely stop and adjust something on the gear of the horse or Hercule's uniform, and say a word or make some observations. Then perhaps he could ask permission to speak, and tell him, or he could ask permission to see him in his office the next morning, or he could in the usual routine way ask the lieutenant for permission to talk to the Colonel. Hercule continued with his work and looked very depressed. He said it wasn't necessary to tell the Colonel, especially since Father Martinez did not ask him any more to speak to the Colonel and so why should he. He had a home in the village, and all the things they needed had somehow come. The Killer said: "But if the Colonel does not know, then when he finds out for himself there will be hell to pay. You better tell him." The unhappy father was polishing his Wellington boots, and he stopped and said that he would tell Papa. When inspection time came, Papa walked around the horse, inspected Hercule, and found nothing wrong, and he was in a good mood, but Hercule kept looking straight ahead and said nothing. He said later that he couldn't say anything to the Colonel because the Colonel had said nothing to him, and besides he was at attention. He went, however, to the officer of the day and obtained permission to speak to the Colonel.

Hercule, however, was given a breathing spell. The next day Papa was very busy with preparations for maneuvers.

In the evening there was a meeting of the important society of the tin soldiers and there was also a lot of work with the preparation of the annual military ball. The appointment for the audience was set for the following day. Meantime, the entire regiment was busy advising Hercule what to say and how to act when facing the Lion of Beaufort.

That day of grace for Hercule was a very happy one for us. During the night the Killer had caught a wild boar sow, and as he stopped to finish the animal he saw two tiny baby boars wobbling in the blinding light of his car. They had been about to cross the road with their mother.

He picked them up and put them in the jeep and when he got back he gave them to us. They were very pretty, with stripes like zebras along the sides of their thin bodies, and we fed them and arranged a nest for them in a box in our room. They did not want to go to sleep, but, after grunting for awhile, they looked around them and then with a sudden start ran off in this direction and that, and then they stopped and grunted again, and they did this most of the night. We fed them from a bottle, and they were very friendly and went to sleep during the day with contented grunts.

4. BAL MILITAIRE

AT THIS TIME everybody was busy with the preparations for the Annual Ball. Sometimes at such parties as the Bal Militaire, we saw Mama. She asked to have us brought down before the dinner which preceded the ball, and Sophie and Caroline took us down to the hall where the people sat around at low tables and on sofas, and talked. We were taken from group to group, I making curtsies and Hugo bowing. We were admired in our pajamas and flannel robes, and then with a wave of the hand to the nurses, we disappeared upstairs again.

On this evening there was again the presentation. The military ladies, some more military than their colonel, general, and major husbands, were dressed in silk and with family jewels and beautiful hair-dos. They and their husbands admired us and then we were sent upstairs. The nurses were getting things ready for us to go to bed when I had the idea that the guests should see our two little baby boars. I took one and Hugo the other and we ran downstairs. We showed them to the first people we met, and they had started to admire them when the baby boars began to wriggle loose from us, and, screaming horribly, with cries that cut the air, they raced about the room in figures of eight and in crisscross circles and into this corner and that. The servants fell, the ladies screamed and jumped from their seats, and my mother said to my father: "Why don't you do something?"

The low tables with apéritifs were upset. Father gave orders and called for the Killer, but he had disappeared. A general with many medals, and with courage, tried to catch one of the little animals, but it slipped out of his hands after biting him and got away with more terrible screams. Papa asked again for the Killer—"Qu'il s'occupe de ça," he said. Finally the boars took refuge in the dining room. The doors were closed. The dinner could not be served, and we both stood crying on the stairs and asking for the Killer to come and catch our pets. Papa came and said: "Go upstairs immediately" and said that he would deal with us tomorrow.

It was all very upsetting and Mama at such times got very pale, and her nostrils white and distended. She pulled at her dress here and there, and lit a cigarette, and gave Papa dark looks.

We were pulled up the stairs by Sophie and Caroline and we tried to keep holding on to the banister for we wanted our pets. Upstairs finally we were put to bed, but were hardly in bed when we were taken downstairs again, since one of the officers had the brilliant idea that we might be able to catch the boars. We went into the dining room. The two little animals sat under a table and we had no trouble picking them up, and then, through the kitchen and up the backstairs, and back to our rooms.

Sophie and Caroline said that by tomorrow Papa would have forgotten all about it, and they kissed us good night, and the boars lay exhausted in their box.

Papa, however, had not forgotten, and we were commanded to be at his office at ten the next day.

Brushed, washed, and combed, we were brought down to Papa's study. He sent Caroline and Sophie away. It smelled elegantly of his perfumed cigarettes, of the flowers on his desk, of his boots, and of all the things that make a room like this a frame for the person who lives in it. There was a great desk with a signed picture of Marshal Foch, a statue of Napoleon on the mantelpiece, several prints of soldiers in uniform. All was neat and nothing unnecessary.

We stood there and Papa asked us to sit down on the leather sofa. He started to make a speech, and then he began a cross-examination. We did not give the Killer away. We said we got the boars in the barn near the stable —some soldiers had them. We didn't remember which ones—the time we didn't remember or how long we had them, and all the details bored us. Then came the question of who had decided on taking them down. I said that I had. "Why?" "Oh, to amuse the guests and to show them to the people." He made another speech and then put his cigarette away, and he said:

"And now, so that you will remember never to do anything like that again"—with this he got hold of me, by the neck of my dress. He did not exactly know how to proceed as he had never done it before. He pulled me toward him and put me over his knee, lifted my skirt and smacked me hard.

I had never been hit before except in play and I was suddenly taken with fury and I cried:

"Let go you swine!"

"Assassin!"

"Dirty skin of a cow!"

"Polichinelle!"

I exhausted the entire repertory of the soldiers when they argued amongst themselves, complained, or called my father names.

He stood me on my feet. He got red in the face, lost control of himself, smacked me twice *paff paff* in the face so that I thought my head would come off.

I looked at him and then I kicked him, and said I wished that he was dead. He took his stick and said he would teach me how to speak to one's father, and he thrashed me with it. I had some more words like "Martinet," and "Kangourou," and a favorite expression of the soldiers which went:

"Allez-vous faire enculer par les Cosaques."

He screamed: "What did you say to me?"

He shook me, he was breathing hard. I did not cry but my brother did. It never came into my father's head that we had no idea of the meanings or weight of the words which we had picked up in the stable. He beat me until he was exhausted.

He slapped my brother's face *paff paff* but he did not beat him then.

He called Mama on the phone and accused her of having neglected our upbringing and he said that he would now take care of it himself before it was too late.

He told my brother to report the next morning in the office at ten, and he dismissed us as if we were soldiers. He saw that my nose was bleeding and called me to him, and with his handkerchief smelling of lavender he dried my nose. I got hold of his stick and broke it and threw it on the floor, but he did not hit me again. He said that he would either break us, or make us—and to be back at his office the next morning at ten.

"I will show you, I will teach you. You shall get to know the other side of me. I will deal severely with you from this day on."

He handed me the bloodstained handkerchief and I threw that on the floor also. In the corridor outside the office we saw Hercule approaching.

Poor Hercule had chosen the worst moment to inform his colonel of the fact that he was married to Sophie without permission and that they had a baby. The Colonel asked him a few questions about when that all had happened and then screamed with rage—that no wonder things were as they were with us, and that it was inadmissible to have a girl in his employ as nurse for his children who was little better than a common whore. He said she was dismissed as of the hour, and was not to come near us. With Hercule he would deal severely later, and also he would see about Father Martinez, who was unfit and irresponsible. Then he went out to the regiment, and his officers and men had a terrible day.

We reported the next day as told. Papa had a new stick, and we both got a thrashing for no particular reason.

Hercule got off easier, for he was needed for the parade, and whenever I hear the triumphal march from "Aïda," and the strains of the "Sambre et Meuse" I get a pain in my backside, for these two pieces were being rehearsed by the mounted band while we received our beatings on those two days at ten in the morning.

5. THE RIDING LESSON

PAPA WAS a military perfectionist, and when something was not right he took charge.

His officers feared him at such times, and the men then called him the worst names, for he was there, every unexpected moment, stick or whip in hand, and his face stony, and he snapped commands, and these had better be obeyed instantly or else there was punishment.

"What I have said I have said" was the constant refrain. There was no appealing his decisions. Now he had decided that we needed straightening out. Sophie had been discharged, and she had to leave immediately. Caroline was to take care of both of us until a new governess, and a proper one, would arrive. In the meantime Caroline had a fearful time, for Papa came into the nursery, had everything shown him, everything unpacked. He inspected every corner, every drawer, the conditions of the toilet, of the windows. The beds had to be moved, the mattresses taken off the beds and aired. He neglected himself, taking time from his morning preparations, and had upset his whole routine to repair the damage done us by letting us grow up like savages. My brother and I were separated. Caroline was sent to help in the kitchen.

A tutor arrived for Hugo, and a governess for me. The third day the governess slapped me without taking off her rings. I had no one to go to complain to. Papa, pointing at me with his stick, said that now a new wind was blowing and that he would straighten us out or know the reason why. I stuck my tongue out at him and he thrashed me again, and then demanded that I apologize, and I said that he could kill me, but I would never apologize to him. So there was more punishment. No joy, no hope, no kisses from Sophie or Caroline. The barracks and the soldiers were forbidden us, and except for the Killer who sneaked me some candies, there was no friendly face.

At this time my little brother fared worse than I, for Papa took him in hand completely, quartering him close to his office, and instead of rolling in the grass, or riding with Hercule on the immense gray Percheron, the Grand Romulus which carried the kettledrums, he was always with his tutor.

Among the numberless quarters in the vast château, there was a small house built on top of the castle, high up, and outside it a terrace, overlooking the parade ground. Directly below this was a small riding ring, like a little bull ring, with a wooden barrier around it. It was used to school horses, and to calm down Papa's charger before he mounted it.

I was put into this place with the new governess. There was a long stone walk with endless stairs before one came up there, and on the stone balustrade that surrounded the terrace there were flowerpots with withered geraniums in

them. In one, a large one, was a cactus plant, which near
the soil was the color of leather and the rest a dead pale
green and yellow with dried spines sticking from it. Whenever I could I came to the balustrade to look down and
out, and I saw the Killer pass, and wave, and smile up at
me. There was also Caroline carrying a basket of linen
and she looked up and started to cry when she saw me.
Then one morning, after I was washed and my hair pulled
by a tight comb, I heard my father's voice below. I ran
out to look down and there was my brother with a horse
whose name was the Black Turk, and Papa, with a whip.
He was giving Hugo a riding lesson. There was no saddle
on the horse. Papa lifted Hugo onto the horse, and then
he took a coin from his pocket and placed it under Hugo's
seat and he told him to see to it that the coin stayed there,
that is, to keep sitting down hard on the horse. Then he
gave him the reins and instructed him how they were to
be held. Then he clicked his tongue and said to Hugo to
get going. Hugo made some motions which were all wrong,
and Papa started to talk to him as he did to recruits, berating everything about him and making him nervous. He
seemed to want to teach Hugo all about riding in one
lesson—and my brother had been only on the Grand
Romulus, which was like sitting on a couch, and with
Hercule holding him, and going in a slow trot at the most.

Papa was very correct and never used bad language.
When berating someone he used a set of words over and
over again. They were:

Bon sang de bon sang!

Nom de nom!

Crénom de nom!

Sapristi!

Parbleu!

and such expressions—but he shouted them.

Papa screamed: "Clumsy one—Maladroit—pay attention—sapristi—keep your back straight, knees and calves
against the horse—"

Toes out, nom de nom—

Heels down—

Watch your hands, crénom de nom—

Trot, canter, trot, canter, sit down on the horse, jump-
ing jack—

"Now try and make a serpentine if you can. Do you
know what a serpentine is?

"Hands, sapristi!—bon sang de bon sang—what am I
talking to you for?

"Knees, grip the horse with them—keep your head up,
look straight ahead, don't look at me—nom de nom."

Louder and louder, and whip in hand—and now the
horse was excited and breathing heavily, and confused by
the rider and the teacher. It began sweating, and my father
screamed to do over again and over again whatever was
not right. Hugo was near tears, his lower lip hung loose—
he was not as strong a boy as I was a girl. He tried to do
what his father told him, but it was impossible to follow
all commands at the same time. He was stiff with fright,
and I feared that at any moment he would fall off the horse.
My father stood beneath where I was, and slapped his boot
with his whip and screamed and I found all at once the
strength to lift the heavy cactus plant, pot, earth, and all,
and let it go over the parapet. I watched it quickly get
smaller and smaller as it went down, and it hit the ground,
with dust spraying as if from a bomb and with a terrible
thud. The horse shied, but my brother stayed on. My father

looked up, and I stayed where I was looking down at him. He took my brother off his horse and sent him on, and he was up in the tower where I was in a minute. He got hold of me, he was very practiced now, and he shook me and then thrashed me until the hard, new governess could not watch it any more and saying "Enough now" grabbed me from him.

She took me to my room, bathed me, and then put some lotion on me, and she said that my father was insane. I was black-and-blue and had welts from a previous beating. She put me to bed and she said that she was sorry. Papa came and said that he had decided to send me into a convent school in Beaufort. He said it was something he should have done long ago.

6. PÊCHE MELBA

IT STARTED like a funeral. It was a cold morning at the beginning of winter, and the castle and the trees were as if painted with wet blue ink—when I left.

The Killer was there and beside him sobbing, stood Sophie, who was here because my parents had gone away. She had her baby in her arms, and there was Caroline, in tears, holding me by the hand and kissing me, and stroking my hair. Auguste, the deaf chauffeur, who also was about to weep, finally took my valise and said:

"Come, we must go."

And he put me into the car and then sitting beside me started the motor. There was a last good-by, and then we drove out the gate past the stables and I felt as if I had a stone in my stomach. The band was mounting, a soldier toodled a good-by on his trumpet, and Hercule waved at me from aboard the Grand Romulus—and then we drove into Beaufort.

And there, in a street of gray walls, the car stopped. We got out. There was a door and a bell. Auguste rang it and a nun looked out through the grating of a small window at the side of the door. The door opened and we were let in. My little bag was given to the nun. I found myself among curious children in blue dresses and black aprons. I looked for the chauffeur but he was gone. My heart sank low. When one is small one has a terrible fear of being an orphan and having no parents, and therefore does not like orphans. I thought that these were orphans whom we had sometimes seen walking on the street, and felt great pity for, but no kinship.

The court was neither garden nor square. There was ground, earth black and wet, trees without leaves and without branches that had been clipped and had large knobby heads. The four sides of the court were enclosed by walls, the roof of a chapel rose to the sky like a tooth in a giant saw, and up above was the sky, a gray darkening cheerless sky, and birds borne by the wind sailed over the roofs like kites without strings to hold them.

The children stood around me and looked at me with curiosity. They were all sad, bundled up in various scarves. I now saw there were two kinds of children, those in the blue dresses and black aprons, and others dressed in individual clothes. These latter were the lucky ones, for they were called for and taken home toward evening. I hoped I would be among them.

Then a nun came and took me inside the convent to the room of the Mother Superior, who was called Mère Ursule. She was a small woman with a thin, narrow jaw and a strong nose. Like everyone here, she looked as if she were ill. Other nuns came and looked at me. Nobody smiled.

In the stables back home there was a place where dry sacks were hung and grain was kept. There mice lived, and the smell of those dry sacks and the droppings of mice, which has a sweet smell, was the same as the sweat and the various ointments those old nuns used for their rheumatism and ills.

Going into the cloister was like being on a train that entered a dark tunnel. The walls everywhere were painted a dark brown up to the height of my head, and on them ran lines which the children had scraped as they walked along.

The nuns in black habits and long black head coverings floated along like big black birds trailing their wings. The windows were painted halfway up so that one could not see out or in. It was all half dark. The room in which we slept had little iron beds along the wall and dark brown linoleum on the floor. This linoleum was torn in the way linoleum tears and patched with pieces tacked one above the other in irregular shapes, with bits of string at the ends and cracks along the edges. The wooden toilet was for several people and had a row of six small circular openings with round wooden covers on them. The washstand was also wooden and chipped porcelain basins were set in it in rows. The soap was brown, the toilet paper was cut-up newspaper held together by pieces of string.

One came to the chapel after passing through a long corridor, again painted brown. It was dimly lit by small windows near the ceiling. One could barely see. Halfway down was a gate that opened to the choir stalls reserved for the Sisters. There they sang for hours, or rather jammered in a high whining chorus, and said endless litanies and confessed themselves to a bent priest, who fitted in with them and smelled the way they did.

In the dining room stood long tables with small chairs

for the children and one table with big chairs for the nuns. There was no linen but just oilcloth over the wood, heavy crockery, and tin mugs for milk. Everything seemed covered with a coat of grease made of old age and sadness.

In the kitchen, among those who worked with their hands, were the younger nuns, but in spite of their youth they already had the marks of the older ones on them.

They were unloved women, hiding their ugliness behind these walls and in the mummery of the Penitent Order. Soon they would be cobwebbed with misery like the others. Now unsmiling, they would soon become suspicious, watching each other and speculating who of them mortified herself the most. They seemed to take a dose of poison every morning. They went to church with tapers in the dark mornings, their breath rising in vapor with ours as we prayed. It was all mildewed and the corridors forever echoed to coughs.

The first night, after I waited in vain for Auguste to return, I lay in my bed and waited and waited for the bell to ring, and I thought that perhaps Papa would come and take me back but I would say "Thank you—I like it very much here" and send him away, and I would die here of lonesomeness and dirt, and from vomiting food and hating nuns and the priest.

There was no bath before going to bed. I lay awake a long time and then I dreamed of the Killer, and the animals he found in the forest, and of the soldiers and the mounted band, of the good Père Martinez. The night became my only friend.

The most terrible thing was waking up. There was no hope. I had been left alone a few days to get used to the place; then I received the ugly uniform and uncouth heavy shoes, and the rules were told me. It began with the first waking moment. I knew all the nuns now and they had all faces of reptiles, of ugly birds—of rodents to me—and ugly hands with awful scaly gray nails like the claws of a hawk.

The first thing upon rising was to lie prone and kiss the floor, and when I refused to do this I was taken to the little Mother Superior. She fixed me with her bird stare and screeched at me. She said she demanded absolute obedience without exception, and that I now prostrate myself before her and kiss the floor. She sat in a chair in front of me and she pointed at the floor with a bony finger and she yelled, "Instantly, and here, you get down and do as I tell you." Her mouth worked with the lips pressed together. She looked at me, I looked at her and when I said that never, never would I get down on the floor, and certainly never on this dirty floor, she came forward out of her chair, and smacked me in one practiced motion—left-right left-right—with both sides of her hand.

I jumped at her and grabbed her by the throat above the white stiff collar of her habit.

At this the Sisters almost fainted. Two tried to pull me off, the others cried out and reached in the air and for their hearts, and crossed themselves and yammered. I let go of her. She was paler than usual and her thin mouth worked again, and now one of the nuns was able to speak and she said that I had committed a mortal sin. She was a vulgar person from around the neighborhood, judging by the way she spoke. She had pronounced the word *péché*, which is for sin, like *pêche*, which is for peach, and I said:

"Yes, pêche Melba, tarte aux pêches, compote of peaches, peach ice cream, vanilla ice cream, chocolate ice cream, chocolate soufflé, tarte aux pommes, and tarte aux cerises—damn you all, old skins of cows and to hell with you, let yourself be enculé par les Cosaques."

"Out with her, out with her, out of my sight with this creature," screeched the Monster Mother Superior.

They all were in a state of terrible excitement and the priest was called. He came limping in and blinked also like a half-dead old bird.

"What happened?"

He was told the things he could be told.

"That is the one—there."

"Yes, that is the one," they said, and he looked at me, but I think he knew that he had better not touch me and he said:

"Shame—shame on you—"

He gave a long lecture and said that my parents would be informed and that it was a disgrace that a child of such family as mine behaved as I did, and to put me in a room by myself so that I would not spoil the others—the good children. And so I found myself separated from the group and I went to bed without supper, which was no particular punishment here as the food stank, like everything, of poverty, and there never was any dessert—and that is why I had read off the litany of peaches Melba, and pie and soufflés, for certainly the God who let peaches and plums grow, did not want them not to be eaten.

I had to remain in my room, which also had a window painted halfway up. I pulled the bed to the window and tried to open it, and then I started to think seriously on how to break it open and get out and over the wall, or through the door . . . to say good-by to the sad trees, the sad children with their pale faces, the watery soup, the milk from an ugly pitcher running bluish into the tin cups, and the sad nuns and the ugly hands with which they prayed.

I climbed up to the window sill. There was a puddle in the yard outside, in which the sky reflected itself, now beautifuly blue in the mirror in the center of all this dusty place. Then this blue patch came alive with roaring planes. Then there was more excitement, they talked about the Germans coming and the nuns trembled at this thought and what would happen to them, and then Auguste was there—and I ran out, and he put his arms around me. Papa had gone to war, Mama and Hugo and I would go to visit Grandmother in Spain and we would stay there until the trouble was over.

Caroline washed me and did my hair and cried. Hugo had become a different boy. He was not like the brother he had been. He sat still at table, he behaved. I behaved, we were both like grownups. The Killer shook his head.

Mama announced that we were invited to a birthday party for Colonel de Voltera's daughter Veronique. The Colonel was in the same division as my father, and very well liked, social and well off, and he also had a boy named Alain who was two years older than Hugo. The girl Veronique was my age.

Normally we would have said no to such an invitation but now we did anything to get out of the house and away from Mama. The chauffeur drove us over. Alain was a very handsome boy, full of himself and very proud. He loved his sister very much, however, and was always near her.

We were playing blind man's buff in the garden and running and amusing ourselves, when suddenly all became quiet. I took off the blindfold to see why all was quiet, and it was on account of the parents of the de Voltera children. They had walked into the garden. It was exactly like at home. They looked at us the way our parents did.

Colonel de Voltera said: "Go on, go on with the game," but it didn't help.

Madame de Voltera asked me the questions that every such woman asks a child:

"How old are you, oh you are the same age as Veronique, how nice—" and so on—so I curtsied, and we waited until they left before playing again. Then I asked Veronique:

"Does your father beat you?"

"Yes, of course, even today on my birthday."

"And does he beat your brother?"

She nodded as she put the blindfold on me, and later she told me that her father whipped Alain almost every day, but that Alain had learned to pull the muscles of his backside tight and then it did not hurt so much, and one could stand a lot of it. This broke the ice and we went into the salon. There were balloons.

"Try it," she said, blowing up a balloon. I took a balloon to blow up. She said:

"No, I mean try stiffening your behind when you get beaten. It helps, that's true."

There were gay colors, a large buffet, and a dozen guests besides the two Voltera children, and Veronique said:

"You know, I have discovered something. Come with me and see."

She took me to the nursery, and there in a very beautiful crib with baby blue satin, white lace, and ribbons all over lay a new little brother, three months old. He was sleeping on his stomach and Veronique said "Watch," and she put her hand over the baby's skull and slowly squeezed, and the head of the baby gave, like a rubber ball.

"Come and try it," she said, and I did, and it was a curious feeling. Then Hugo came into the room, and with his strong hand he squeezed, and then all the others tried it and whenever we came to the Voltera's house, we went to the nursery and when the nurse was busy we talked to the baby and squeezed his head. He did not cry, he smiled happily, and he died a few years later. And so there was only Alain and Veronique—and Hugo and I. We were very good friends.

7. THE WILD ASPARAGUS

WE SAW THE BLUE BOATS of St.-Jean-de-Luz, then the hats
of the Spanish soldiers, and there was heat, sun, large free
hills, and then the city and my grandmother's house whose
door consisted of a small door set in a large one, and over
it the biggest stone coat of arms I have ever seen. There
was a large courtyard inside where for awhile you could
see nothing because the light outside was so intense. A few
people in long coats sat in the patio and they did not
turn their heads to look at us. A dog came, big, but so light
so thin he seemed to be dancing suspended in air like a
marionette. He had a very beautiful head.

My grandmother looked like my mother: a long nose and
a pale face, black hair, and it was as if she forever sat for
her portrait. There were tiled floors with here and there
a rug, and a very big butler named Luis; silver candelabra,
and furniture as in a church, portraits in big frames of
people who looked like my mother and grandmother and
all proud—nobody seemed very gay. The eyes were dark
and there was something curious about them. They were

set very close together and were goatlike in their way of looking and in their fixed intense stare. They were different from any people I had seen except perhaps Mama.

Grandmother changed her pose and allowed herself to be kissed by Mama, and then by Hugo and myself. The butler brought something that looked like pastry but instead was olives and anchovies cooked with oil. Politely we took one of each and then said thank you. It all smelled of oil—people, dog, cat, which was skinny, and small kittens, which cried and their bones stuck out.

The butler kicked the dog who had received most of my and half of Hugo's olive and anchovy pastry. In my room, the dark bed, the floor, all smelled of oil.

We were taken around the city in an automobile that belonged to Grandmother—a very old and heavy open car, which had her crest embroidered on the back seats, one on each seat, and this upholstery was new, and we were told to be very careful, and not put our feet on it. Then we saw a statue of Carlos III, who also looked like a goat, the churches, and then the bull ring. Mama pointed all this out to us, along with the heavily becrested houses where the friends and relatives of the family lived, and it still all smelled of oil.

When we came back, a light passed over Grandma's face. She straightened the ribbon in my hair and said that she was happy I had come to celebrate my First Communion, and she was very proud of this, and that the special instructions that I would need would be given me by a very fine man, a priest who was a relative.

Monsignor Felice was also goat-faced, with eyes burning as if he had fever. He was very tall, very thin, and walked with long strides, so that his soutane flew after him this way and that. He could never stand still, he constantly had his hands together and apart and talked very vividly, and as he sailed back and forth in front or in back of me, he never took his intense eyes from my face and my person. He examined me from head to foot. The lessons started soon, and dresses were ordered. The seamstress to make them came to the house, and it was all busy and centered about me, for the First Communion would take place at the Fiesta.

There was much lace. Grandma wanted me dressed like the portrait of an infanta which hung in one of the salons. I had inherited a dark hue of skin and she said I would be the most beautiful of all the children at Communion. The lessons were taken in a small room where I was alone with Monsignor Felice.

He spoke of Grandmother as the Condesa. He was very busy with preparations for the Feria, and the feast of the penitents. His eyes burned into me. Sometimes he took me on his lap and he had his hand on my shoulder and patted me, and he kissed me when I left. He never took his eyes off me. At table where he ate like a wolf, quickly and nervously, he looked at his plate, and quickly here or there, and then his gaze came to me again. He told my mother that I was the most beautiful child he had ever seen, and that such beauty was fatal to people. He spoke of my great classical beauty to everyone and embarrassingly so, in detail: my eyes, the oval shape of my face; my body, its proportions, the tallness, the slim calves, the fine long fingers; my poise and proud bearing; and he always said that unless one as beautiful as I was had a great deal of strength of character and discipline and, above all, faith, she would be unhappy, for the world was a wicked place, and danger lurked everywhere.

He spoke French for our benefit, and he told funny stories in French, at which everyone laughed, including the butler who did not understand one word of the language. But that is Spanish politeness. The dining room was immense and it smelled of heliotrope and Chanel No. 5, which was Grandmother's perfume, and which she must have sprayed on herself like a shower. Servants seemed to come out of the wall whenever one needed them and we lived by the moon rather than the sun, for luncheon was at four, and dinner at eleven, and we went to bed in the middle of the night. At meals a servant stood behind each chair, and there the second day I saw a woman who was uglier than any I had seen so far. She had a face like a dead fish, but not one with scales, a fishskin fish, dark and bluish, the eyes in sockets close to the huge nose, the face full of lines going this way and that, and around the mouth, from the nose down, most of them spread like an open fan. Her teeth were such as I never saw again outside of Spain: they did not belong in a human face at all. She was so terrible-looking that the well-trained servants made faces when they approached her, not in amusement, but in fright, as you would going near something very hot, or some animal that might bite. My mother and my aunt and this fearful lady, who was a duchess, always played bridge after lunch, together with a fourth lady who was a princess and very fat with much jewelry and spots on her face, back, and neck.

Don Felice, who said the prayer at table, always started

with his hand on my head, or on my shoulder, or on my arm:

"Praise be to God the beneficent King, the Creator of the Universe who hath raised the Heavens without pillars and spread out the Earth as a bed—"

He said this close to my face, smelling of oil, of garlic. They were all slow and deliberate eaters: the white-gloved servants reached for the golden plates that were on the table when one sat down at four, and it was dark outside when they pulled the chairs, and it was torture twice a day. There was nothing interesting said, and the entertainment was to look at the face of the Duchess and shiver and think oh what ugliness is possible on this small planet that is the human face. She had a voice that went with it, and with this she said to me:

"What are you staring at me for?" and so this was also over and I had much trouble keeping my eyes averted. Then Don Felice told a story in Spanish, and the Duchess laughed and threw her head back and I looked at her again. She showed all her frightening teeth, the roof of the mouth, the gray tongue, and her nostrils into each of which one could stick a pack of fingers. She looked at me suddenly and said:

"I thought I told you not to stare at me." I apologized, and she gave me a deadly look.

Another guest at table was a French count, a very quiet and old gentleman whom they called Pistache, who occasionally smiled at me with sympathy. He would look at the old Duchess and then make faces, so that I had to laugh out loud and, once, having a mouthful of green peas, they came out over the table like bird shot. I was told to leave the table, but I liked the Count very much. He told stories

that were funny, and he looked at me while he told them as
if saying, "I know you are bored to death—this is especially
for you." It was good, however, that I had laughed at the
Count, for from then on Hugo and I ate separately in another dining room and were served by a very kind woman,
and we could refuse most dishes and just pick out what
we liked and what didn't smell of oil, and that was very
little.

There were, however, always again the terrible sessions
when Don Felice sent for me, and he would come close
to me, saying his lessons and instructions, and breathing
the menu on me. I leaned away and I tried to hold my
breath, but he followed me with his face, and eventually I
had to open my mouth and it was like swallowing everything he had eaten at one gulp.

Afterward we went down, and there would be a new
visitor or several, and he would again describe my beauty,
adding something new. He said that one could not expect
anything but such beauty when one looked at the Condesa
and Mama, and the sharpest intelligence also, and that all
the good fairies had stood at my crib, but that there was
also the Devil. His eyes burned hottest when he spoke of
the Devil, his voice rose; it was as if one pressed another
key, the deepest on the organ; it came out of his nose
rather than his mouth alone; it rang, and both Grandmother and Mama looked at me then, together with him,
and they trembled with the kind of excitement you have in
the theater.

Monsignor had a large ring which they kissed, and when
he came into the room he stepped from between the two
tapestries that masked the entrance to the great hall like an
actor in a drama, with folded hands; he came forward and

his smile of arrival was not a smile at all, it was a very serious grimace. He ate at the house every day. Grandmother did nothing without consulting him. I did my religious lessons and searched my soul every day as he commanded. Hugo had it better, he had made friends with the concierge's boy and he played. They had a wooden contraption like a wheelbarrow, with a painted wooden bull's head on it, and a red piece of cloth, and the boy showed Hugo how to avoid the bull.

The concierge's boy and his little sister were always happy. They had parents who loved them very much. The parents had endless patience with them, lifted them up and kissed them, and looked at them with much love; never were they punished, and I felt very happy for them. My brother and I were like birds that flew against walls and windows when we tried to get someone to love us. How fortunate it was to be the child of poor people and of ordinary folk.

The Spaniards were very nice to children everywhere. They were bad with animals. I asked Monsignor why once during a lesson. He took a religious book in which there were illustrations and he said, pointing at a picture of a man and a woman, that these were creatures that had a soul and one had to be very careful about men's souls— and that there was everlasting life for the soul, but that animals had no souls and no feelings. It didn't matter much what was done to them. They were for the use of man and when one saw a donkey beaten, it was to make the lazy beast walk.

He walked up and down the room explaining the need of discipline and order in all things, sailing back and forth and talking, as he did in church, with authority, as my father talked to recruits and officers whom he always dismissed with an arrogant final sentence that went:

"Ce que j'ai dit, j'ai dit—"

and with soldiers he added:

"Never will I change anything I have said. Remember that. Out! Go!"

Only Papa was better with animals. If he had been as good to us as he was with horses and dogs, we would have had a glorious life.

Monsignor took walks with me. We visited convents and churches. Secretly I thought that he was the Devil— the Devil smelling of oil, garlic, and incense, rather than sulfur and brimstone.

Every day he dwelt on hellfire and purgatory, and he always stopped in front of terrible pictures depicting scenes of fire and torture. Also he pointed out every statue on churches that had to do with the Devil, gargoyles and cloven-hoofed creatures. Then he looked more goaty and evil than the pictures and Devils he pointed at, and I tried to banish the thought from my mind that he was the Devil himself. I was afraid that he could read these thoughts from my face, for he was always searching me, and always questioning me about what I was thinking.

After endless tryons and changes the dress for the First Communion was finished. It was very beautiful and I was photographed in it. Grandmother also wanted me to be painted but she said there was no longer any painter to do it, and Monsignor agreed with her.

The city was decorated all over and the streets filled with people in their best clothes, and there were tents and stands where wine, shrimps, and cakes would be sold, and large copper caldrons were set up and heated.

In the house was quiet and darkness. The dog got most of our food under the table.

On the first day of the Semana Santa we were allowed up late. On both sides of the coat of arms in front of the house were large balconies of wrought iron. One of the balconies was arranged for Grandmother and us with elaborate chairs, draperies, and carpets. The other one was for the household.

Monsignor Felice stood in back of me, and when the procession began, he told me to stand on the chair to see better, and so that I would not fall he held me, with one arm across my body, and he pointed out things and explained them.

The music began, and hooded penitents with eyeslits, carrying long candles, walked behind a mounted troupe clad in very beautiful costumes, blowing on silver trumpets; after them a Madonna with many many candles and jewels, and tears in her eyes and on her cheeks, carried by other penitents who crouched under the float on which she stood.

Then came "Cabezudos," figures with immense heads like idiots, a figure in a cocked hat and with a staff, a Moor in a white turban, then a tribe of giants with long, wooden arms swinging at the sides of their immense bodies.

The giant figures of a king and queen which were Ferdinand and Isabella were swaying and dancing, and then a lot of giant people, fat and gross, all dancing to fife and drum music, and around them all the children of the town. There came statues representing Religion and Faith, and others who were meant to be Africa, America, Asia, and Europe. Also a hideous figure that was an animal like a dragon, and made terrible sounds. It roared and shook, and came very close to us on the balcony with its ugly face. I got scared and held on to Monsignor Felice, who took me into both his arms and said not to be afraid. There were more statues of Madonnas with jewels pinned to them, and candles. It lasted a long time, and afterward we ate shrimps and drank wine and went to bed.

The next day, the street was blood red from the shells of millions of shrimps that had been eaten, and there was the smell of burning oil from caldrons in which an endless kind of dough sausage pressed from a metal squeeze gun had been cooked.

I was told by Grandmother that there would be my most important confession on Saturday, for which Monsignor Felice would come to the chapel at the house, and then on Sunday, Communion. I was looked upon by all as if I were a holy statue. My mother and grandmother were in constant prayer.

On the day before the confession, Grandmother took us in the car to drive out to her estate, where there was a chapel with her patron saint, and in which she wanted to pray. As we drove up a hill on the way back, she saw a boy in the field with an armful of greenery, and she stopped the car and called him. The boy had been picking wild asparagus which is very thin and long.

The boy came to the car and Granmother asked him his name, and asked if he came often to steal people's property. The boy had no answer: he looked frightened. Don Felice had gotten out of the car and stood looking at the boy and he read him a lecture. The little boy looked very sad as Don Felice took the large bunch of asparagus from him. Grandmother asked the boy where he lived and he pointed down the road. The little boy was asked to get in the car and Grandmother said that she would tell his mother about the theft of her wild asparagus. He was told to sit at the other side of Monsignor. I was in one of my new dresses, up front with the chauffeur. We drove on, and after awhile Don Felice whispered something to Grandmother, and she asked the chauffeur to stop the car. It smelled horribly and the little boy was let out. He had been so scared that he had done something in his trousers and there was a large stain on the beautiful upholstery. Grandmother made a remark about "These dirty animals" and she put some perfume on a handkerchief and held it to her nose.

I was very happy for the little boy—who had lost the asparagus which Don Felice had given to the chauffeur—for he had gained his freedom. The little boy ran across the fields as quickly as he could with his stick-thin legs. If only I could run away like that from tomorrow.

After the chauffeur tried to get the stain removed, we drove on. Don Felice said it was better to let it dry and then have it properly cleaned.

My grandmother took Don Felice's hand and, taking the lace handkerchief from her nose, she said with a grateful look at him that she wouldn't know what to do without him.

He made a curious face, and looked at me as people do who share a secret joke.

8. THE SPANISH CONFESSION

THE NEXT DAY was Saturday and finally the dreaded hour was here. My mother and my aunt, both in dark, rustling silk, went into the chapel, respectfully following Don Felice, and I in back of them. They went with me to the altar and prayed, while the priest went into the sacristy to change his vestments and put on his stole. Then he installed himself in the confessional, and when he coughed, my grandmother, aunt, and mother crossed themselves and left the chapel. I went to the confessional, and I saw his eyes burning on me again, and then he closed the velvet curtain in front of him. I saw part of his face in a beam of light, through the grating that separated us. Most of him was in the dark corner in which he leaned. He bent forward and inclined his ear toward me. I said as is demanded:

"Bénissez-moi, mon Père, parce que j'ai péché—"

There was a silence; then came the moment when one begins, stretched now, and becoming longer and longer.

Don Felice leaned close against the grating and whispered:

"Mon enfant, je vous écoute. . . ."

I could not speak. He continued:

"Have you nothing to say to me, my child?"

I said: "No, I have nothing to say to you."

"You are to make your First Communion tomorrow, and I must point out to you that you will be in a state of mortal sin if you do so without first confessing."

I said: "Ça m'est égal—I am judge of my sins, judge of my acts, and of my faults."

It was not a question of being ashamed of my sins, but of confessing myself to someone I knew well enough not to have any respect for. I said to him that nobody could forgive my sins except myself; I was big enough to know what I did that was good and what was evil, and that I could not confess myself to him.

He whispered: "You know, my child, all the sins we commit float upward to God, and He forgives them no matter how bad we have been, and you will feel so much better after confessing. I am merely the messenger, who helps you to search yourself and who presents the sins to our Lord."

I said: "I think I can do that myself—better."

He changed his voice, and talking as he did when speaking of the Devil, he said: "Be humble!" but then he changed his voice again—and whispered: "Oh you are so young, my child, and so headstrong, and you do not understand religion. Now tell me your sins—start with them—and don't be afraid. The first time it will be difficult but later on it will be like a great friendship."

He leaned forward and said:

"Je vous attend, mon enfant. Now make your confession—"

I could not very well tell him that I thought he was the Devil so I said simply:

"Oui, mon Père—I have forgotten to say my morning prayers today, and yesterday my evening prayers."

"That is all you have to confess, my child?"

"Yes."

"Search your soul—is that truly all?"

"Oui, mon Père."

He paused and then said wearily:

"Very well—c'est très bien, mon enfant—you are a very very good child—one must not let oneself be stained by vices. You are sure you have nothing else to confess? For example, have you eaten anything forbidden on the fast day?"

"No, mon Père. I hardly can eat anything here—I couldn't have committed that sin."

"Well good, then I will give you absolution—but I think we will have some sessions together. I must be certain and convinced that you are as pure as you are and that you do not lie to me, which is also a deadly sin."

There was fasting that night. Grandmother's fine car, from which the stains had been removed and which was decorated with white flowers, stood in front of the house. We rode to a very special, flower-filled church and there, with some girls from other families like ours and with long ceremony, I waited to take First Communion. Monsignor Felice officiated.

It is a rule that one closes one's eyes while receiving the Sacrament. When he came to me, I took the wafer on my tongue and I kept looking straight at him, and if he could read my eyes, he could see there that I wanted to say it all counted for nothing between me and my God. There was luncheon and celebration at home. Don Felice behaved as if nothing had happened that was extraordinary, and he praised my beauty and intelligence to the relatives and friends who had not before met me, and he said what a good child I was. There were some traditional foods, and some hard-boiled eggs and bread which was what Hugo and I ate. I had to kiss the terrible face of the Duchess and all the others.

9. THE BULLFIGHT

AFTER THE SIESTA we all got into the car again and went to the bullfight. Grandmother had said that it was not bad and I would enjoy it. Grandmother—who like all the ladies, even I, wore a mantilla when we were in the car—said to the ancient French Count that her whole day was spoiled— hopeless Sunday. She had just found that, while decorating the rooms for my First Communion, one of the servants had nailed a branch of greenery through the tapestry to the wall, driving the nail with a hammer right through the cloth.

"Did you ever hear of anything like that?" she asked of the Duchess, who sat with Grandmother in the back of the car. The Duchess shrugged her shoulder and said:

"Did you speak to him?"

Grandmother said:

"No—what is the use, but I gave the major-domo a calling down. He is a good man, but once a year I give him a lecture, and I hate to. So when this thing with the nail happened, it was time again and I said: 'Listen to me, Luis.

You are very nice, you are very clean always, and you are honest. Those are great qualities in a servant and what more can one ask. Well, one can ask that you pay a little attention, and look after what others do, like nailing branches of greenery through priceless tapestry to the wall. It is your job to direct them. Then you can pay a little more attention to the table. See that the glasses are filled, that the plates are warm, but not so hot they burn people's hands, that the things are passed around properly, that the chairs are pulled out. And while we are on this subject,' I said to him, 'do you know why you have no time to attend to your work properly? Because you listen to the conversation of the guests and you laugh at the jokes. Now don't listen to the conversation, and pay attention to your work. The conversation is not interesting anyway.' Do you know what he said?—He said: 'You are right, Señora la Condesa, the conversation is not very interesting.' "

The Duchess let out a sound of anguish:

"Well that is what one has for servants today."

"Here we are," said my Grandmother. "Now one would think with all the world having elevators, they would install one in a bull ring—but we shall have to climb."

We climbed up and up, slowly on account of Grandmother and the Duchess. I suddenly got a terrible feeling of misery, and I begged my mother to send me back. She got her wildest goat look in her eyes, and her nostrils went waxen, and she held me by the arm so hard that it hurt; she pinched and said that it was all being done for me, and that it would be inadmissible for to me to leave—"inadmissible" was one of Papa's words.

Grandmother had her own box, high up, with her coat of arms, and I was given a seat up front.

In back there was a buffet, a cask of sherry, and other wines on ice, and several servants. The chauffeur had come along to carry some things for Grandma. There were visitors and new relations, and bowing and kissing, and the Duchess, who sat next to me, looked through opera glasses and pointed out people. Then she looked at me and she must have seen how I felt. She straightened out my mantilla, and said:

"This is your first bullfight?"

I said, "Yes."

"Well," she said, "it's very beautiful, and there is nothing to worry about, one gets used to it very quickly—but the first time, my dear, there is a part when the horse comes on . . ." and she said that she herself had never got used to that. "So when that happens, I don't look. I think about my clothes, or my next dinner party, and that is perhaps what you should do, also—don't look when the horse comes, think about your dolls—or your friends—or your lovely dresses."

I thanked the Duchess, and I thought what a disgrace to be here, to sit in this place and watch what will happen, and why does the good God allow it. I looked back—exit would be difficult—Luis, the butler, stood at the buffet, there were a dozen people all around me. My grandmother was to my left, my mother to my right. I thought if the Killer were here with a gun, and shot the bull right through the head between the eyes as he came in, so that he would drop dead before anything started—that would be a glorious thing, and all these people with their shouts and carnival airs and their Spanish pride could then look at each other stupidly and go home. But the Killer wasn't here. My grandmother looked at me again and showed me another girl in another box, also a First Communion celebrant, close by. She waved to me, I smiled at her. Then my mother started some parrot chatter with a lady in the box next to ours. Then she talked in French to the old French Count, who sat in back of me—she was gloriously happy.

Below, the bull ring sand was being raked, a band played, the seats in the arena were all taken, a very prominent bullfighter was to perform. It was all new and very exciting. The places in the shadow were dark and cool, a trumpet blared. The parade started, and I liked that and the music, and then the matadors took their places and a door opened and the bull came in. He seemed small and he ran into the center of the ring, and one of the men spread a cape at which he ran, and then turned; it seemed very gay, and he looked as if he wanted to play. This went on for some time—when suddenly a man came at the bull and stuck two banderillas into his back. I screamed and turned away. My grandmother shook me by the arm and shouted:

"What is the matter with you, behave yourself"—and she pushed me back into my seat.

The old Count Pistache, who sat in back of me, turned to my mother and said very politely that this spectacle was distasteful to me, and might make me ill—and why not let me go home.

Mama turned her coldest face to him, and with waxen nostrils hissed:

"She stays here."

So the Count put his hand on my shoulder and said that

he was sorry—he didn't care too much for it either, but if one lived in Spain, one had to go to bullfights, and to church, and there was little else to do. Then he said:

"Reflect for a moment—that bull down there has had a marvelous life up to now; now he has fifteen minutes of misery and then it's over. That's not too bad as life goes—I'd settle for that."

The bull was trying to get the first banderillas out of his body, dark blood ran from his back, and now the man came running again with new banderillas, and he went toward the bull. I could not look at it any more and pushed my grandmother aside. The Count got up and let me pass. I ran out of the box, my mother screaming "Come back here." Luis, the butler, ran after me, and then also Grandmother's chauffeur and a policeman.

I ran to a passage under the highest seats as fast as I could, and then down a flight of stone steps that led to another circular corridor, up high still and at the back of the arena. It was all of heavy stones, round and round—and roaring with the voices of the people out front. I heard my mother shout, and more guards ran this way and that.

I came to a space between the seats, where people stood watching: it was a large exit. I squeezed between them to hide and they pushed me forward, thinking I wanted to see better. A trumpet blared, and the man on the horse advanced with his lance pointed at the bull. The bull lifted the horse and almost turned it upside down; it fell, and then men came and with sticks beat the poor horse which was old and half dead, and brought it to its feet.

I pushed my way back and there was, as far as I could see, no one. I ran down the circular corridor, and then I came to a ramp that led downward. I ran down, down, and down—and then I came to a passage on the ground. The music was playing, and I was in a place like a street—with dirt on the floor. One end went into the bull ring toward a heavy double door, painted dark red; the other end led to a large space, like a vault in the castle, of stone, big, and lit up by large windows and also large electric lights, and there were wooden beams overhead. I heard voices of people and I decided to run in there and as I turned that way gates from the arena were opened, and three mules, whipped, and with their legs pounding upward, galloped in past me, dragging the dead bull. A man in a red suit whipped them, they came to a halt, and then a dozen men with bloody aprons unhooked the bull and dragged him to the center of the place and in a moment they each had axes and long knives.

The bull's head was put on a wooden block as if on a pillow and they cut off his ears and gave them to a waiting man who ran with them, and then they all worked together without a word, and they chopped off his head and cut him open and the quivering red flesh was steaming. Two with smaller knives started to skin him, and a boy, barelegged and with a knife, stepped into the bull as it was opened, and he took out the entrails and the stomach and sliced it open, and out of it came a liquid mass of spinach soup that ran all over the floor and mixed with blood, and then I fell into this mess as someone pushed me out of the way.

I felt as if I were drowning in blood, and I saw everything as if it were under water. I was picked up and put on a stretcher and then carried around the space between the arena and the bull ring. It all turned like a huge carousel above me, the thousands of faces looking down on me all filled with pity, men and women pointing and the women clasping their hands—and crying—and asking what had happened.

They cried: "Niña—pobrecita—niña—poor little girl."

The men who carried me were of the lot that had beaten the old horse. I was carried past banderillas stuck in the wooden side of the barrera, and men sharpening the points, and then past bullfighters, and where their capes were hung up. The people shouted in sounds that were like the waves of the sea. In the sky the setting sun gilded a plane very high, very small, and then the men turned right and I was taken inside the infirmary, and placed on a table. Two nuns came and took off my dress and started to wash me. I was naked. It smelled of carbolic solution and on the wall, where my feet were, up where the tiling ended, hung a print of the Madonna in a gilded frame. It was tilted toward me, and was like a mirror; I saw a face reflected, staring down on me. At the angle at which it was I could not make out who it was, it looked like the Duchess, and then when I turned my head, I saw that it was Don Felice who stared at me. Then I saw Luis and my mother come in.

I wished someone would cover me up, but the nurses were still washing me with cold water and I lay there helpless.

"Thank merciful heaven," said Don Felice, "she is not hurt, it could have ended terribly."

The nurses covered me up and cleaned the table, and I was put into one of several small beds. The room was bare.

I was given some medicine from a blue bottle, and then the nurses covered me with several blankets. I was still shivering. My mother stood at the foot of my bed; she looked at me and then turned away. Whenever the door was opened one could hear the music and the shouting. They brought in a matador who had been gored in the thigh, and the doctor cut off his trousers. The matador groaned and called out to the Madonna of the bullfighters to come to his aid.

Then Grandmother's chauffeur came, and some guards, and the French Count. Monsignor Felice asked the doctor how badly the bullfighter was hurt. The doctor spoke French and said to the Count that he was afraid that of the things of which every man has two, he would lose one. The doctor added that he knew a man who had only one and was the father of eleven children. The Count laughed loudly. The bullfighter did not hear it for he was just being given an anesthetic. Don Felice looked at the doctor, smiled his curious smile, and said something in Latin. Outside, the people screamed and cried "Olé"—and then the trumpet gave the signal again for the moment when the bull who was in the arena could be killed.

I got sick and everything came up. Then I was carried out into Grandmother's car and that evening I had fever and I prayed for all the poor dogs and horses and thin cats, and the donkeys and goats of Spain, and also for the little boy with the wild asparagus. I had terrible dreams and cried out but nobody came. That had been the First Communion—the Fiesta and the Bullfight and sad Sunday was gone. I was kept in bed for a week and fed milk soup, which also tastes of oil in Spain.

I was in my bed, which was large enough for five children to sleep in, and there were pillows upon pillows. Overhead the embroidery showed a landscape of great beauty, opal in color, and the embroidery all around in blue and gold draped itself in heavy folds down to the floor; the window curtains matched the baldachin. The walls were covered with yellow Chinese silk, and a thick rug, pale blue like the sky in early morning, covered the floor. On the wall above my pillow there was a huge black ebony cross, with a figure of Christ cut from ivory that had turned brown. At the foot of the bed was a prie-dieu upholstered in petit point. The Sister who was in attendance announced Don Felice. She said that he had inquired every day, he had read Masses, he had prayed for me, for I had had a very dangerous fever, and now grace to God and the good doctor I would be all right again.

He came in silently and stood at the edge of my bed. I was very weak. He patted my hand and asked if there was anything he could do. I shook my head. His eyes burned again. He kneeled down on the prie-dieu, and he folded his hands, and then he prayed loudly, and it was like an actor rather than a priest that he said to God to remove him from temptation.

"I have suffered torture—every day since you came," he said, looking at me. "I cannot get you out of my mind, day or night—I weep in my heart of love for you—oh, what I have suffered since you have come to this house, my angel." He got up, and taking a handkerchief out of his soutane went to the window and blew his nose.

Then he turned to me and said:

"Forgive me."

He stared at me. I looked back at him and withstood his stare while thinking, he is really the Devil. He looked down at his hands after awhile and turned and went out.

He left me alone from then on, he never talked about my beauty again, nor gave me any instruction.

My brother went to every bullfight, and shot birds and cats and squirrels, and he became just a person in the street for me during this time.

I lived within myself.

When I was fourteen we went back to Beaufort. We found that the Killer was still alive, and we were happy he was. He had not changed—he had been promoted, and demoted, and he had been wounded, but he said that he had killed many Germans. We visited Veronique and Alain. They had both grown and Alain was very handsome and proud of himself. He always moved something when he stood: a foot, a shoulder, his head, his hands—it was as if someone inside him was building a statue and trying to make it even more wonderful than it was. He was also always changing the expression on his face, trying to look grown-up and serious. He was very proud of Veronique, who was now a beautiful girl, with lovely bosoms and golden hair.

Papa was in Africa, General de Gaulle in London. It was tolerable living as we did so near to farms—there was enough of eggs and butter and milk. A German lieutenant had kissed Veronique. She had run away, and at home had brushed her teeth for hours, and Alain said darkly that it would have gone very badly for the lieutenant if he had been there, and that since then he never let Veronique out of his sight.

10. THE CHANDELIER

VERONIQUE'S PARENTS and mine had agreed with absolute finality that under the circumstances, the times we lived in, and the kind of girls we were, the only thing to do with us was to send us to a convent school, where there was a strict curriculum, and where girls were turned into young ladies with proper manners. Appeals were of no avail. My father would be absent, my mother unable to cope with me, and the same situation prevailed at the house of the Voltera family. There was no appeal to our mothers.

There are two kinds of mothers, those that side with the children, and those that side with their husbands, and the reason for the latter must be that they choose a husband who is a military man to begin with because they admire discipline. Both Veronique's and my mother said to us that what had to be, had to be, and even had we been the most gentle and obedient children we would have to go. We should not look upon it as punishment. On the

76

contrary, it was an honor to go to that school and a privilege reserved for few.

They themselves had been sent away and had cried in despair for weeks and the same would happen to us, and it would do us good and build our characters. Besides it was the thing to do. The only person we could cling to who showed us love, comforted us, and had sympathy, was the Killer.

We were bored while we waited for the final arrangements to be made. We hung around the empty stables.

Veronique and Alain came over and the Killer showed us new knife-throwing tricks. He made it more complicated than before by throwing at a long distance. He would suspend a tire on a chain from a tree, and set the target in back of it, or train us to hit a moving target with knives and sharp axes.

There was no tennis court and, anyway, no tennis balls were available. The horses had mostly been butchered for food, so there was no riding. Knife-throwing was our only amusement and we became very proficient at it and developed large muscles.

Then finally the day came to leave.

I said to my mother: "I ask you for the last time. Don't send me to the convent. If you do I will burn and tear down the place. I will disgrace you."

Over in the other house, Veronique, who was milder, was in tears. She came over and her brother with her, and when he was alone with me he said:

"Don't worry, I will come to the convent school and get you both out."

In the sewing room numbers were put on my linen, and

then I was packed off and Madame de Voltera came to pick me up. Veronique was in the car. The farewell was as if two sheep were being driven out of one stockade into another. My mother in such moments had a stronger Spanish accent, a harder voice than usual. My mother made no motion toward me and I none to her. As we left, the Killer carried my little black valise to the car.

Veronique and I sat on the back seats bumping along. The road was very quickly used up, the fields and the woods we knew well fled our eyes. The houses and the village passed, and then quickly came the road to the school —this enclosed place which we had often seen at a distance with its steeple and gray slate roof. The new large golden cross over the gate and the inscription thereon now were readable as we stopped.

At the last moment of freedom, Madame de Voltera got out and rang a bell we could not hear, for it was far away and rang up at the main house. Castles hereabout—and this looked like a castle rather than a nunnery—had elaborate wrought-iron gates, through which one could see. This one had an entrance made of solid doors of iron, painted gray, heavy and high, attached with massive hinges to iron columns, and from these a stone wall, too high to climb, went to the left and right. Atop this stone wall were iron staves and stretched between them strands of barbed wire. There was a buzzing sound, the gates opened, and we drove into the place we never had expected to see the inside of.

On entering gates, one always has a first and a last look —it's like going to prison. The first look is when you go in, the last look when you come out. From the moment I entered, I looked for the opportunity for the last look—

on how to get out. The gate could be opened, or climbed; the wall was high, but there was a ladder leaning on a plum tree nearby. The plum tree was heavy with fruit. The gates swung closed and the lock clicked—the car drove up between lines of tall poplar trees, and we came to a stone terrace. There stood a pale nun, smiling, and to her we were turned over. Madame de Voltera kissed Veronique on the forehead and admonished her to be good and that was perhaps why she cried and looked after her as she drove away. I did not remember having ever been kissed by my mother, although she told me often that she loved me very much and that therefore she had to be strict with me.

Next, one is confronted with the creatures that will share your fate, and there is hostility on both sides. Then you search the faces of the professors, who in this case were Sisters, and you look to see which one you will dislike the most. There were none here to turn against immediately. They were all more or less nice, and all of them ladies. In prison it's easier to hate than to love; it allows you to proceed at once. In your planning nothing is so awful as to suddenly have feelings, like saying to yourself, "Oh I can't do this or that, because it would hurt the feelings of Sister Marie Thérèse—or Marie Mathilde." In that case you had better change and join the little sheep, and sit it out and come home the joy of the family with your cheeks pink and your eyes clear, and hand Papa the best marks anybody ever had and get a pat on the head—all of which I didn't need. So then, how do we get out of here? Veronique is a rabbit and quakes at everything. I said to her the first evening, "I am getting out of here tonight."

She said: "Oh, let's just wait a day, until we see. Maybe

it's very nice here, and we have each other—and then we can always decide."

What should we do home—that was even more awful. But I didn't want to go home, I just wanted to run away, anywhere—to get out.

"But we have no money—you must be reasonable—" said Veronique.

So I said: "Well, if you feel like that I am going alone—" so she cried again.

But as I have already said, if one feels sorry for another, and that also goes for oneself, one is done for from the beginning; in fact one is done for the moment one is born. So how do I get out?

"How do you get out?" asked Veronique at the moment I was thinking it, and she said: "Are you going to take your valise?" That is something else. When one flees from a place, one doesn't worry about the toothbrush or flannel robe de chambre; you just take yourself and fly like a bird. I looked out of the window; my room was on the third floor, the drop was too steep. I waited until it was dark, and then I left my room. I had already found out that by walking close to the wall there was no creaking in the small polished pieces of wood that formed the parquet. There the floor was stone, long narrow slabs of white marble. Chandeliers hung in all the halls and in the rooms, but they were all out now, except for an emergency light at the end of the corridor. I had my shoes in my hand, and went down the wide stairway, and waited. There was no sound. I went to the ground floor; I walked along in absolute silence, pressed against the wall. There was the door with a large lock, but the heavy key was in it. I reached for it—and suddenly a voice in back of me said:

"Were are you going, my child?"

I turned. As silent as I a Sister had followed me. I said that I couldn't sleep and that I wanted to go in the garden for air.

She took hold of me by my shoulders. She looked at me very directly but kindly, and she said:

"I know the first days are hard, and especially the first nights. Now go back to your room—and don't do this again, for I would have to report you the next time, and then you would get locked in your room." So I went back to bed and Veronique came to my room, and got in my bed, and she cried until she fell asleep.

The next day they thought we were sufficiently settled to put us in uniform. Also we had to listen to the rules and we were examined by a doctor.

In the play period we found two girls who seemed to be our kind—one can always tell at a glance. One of them told me that it was impossible to escape, and if one got away, as they once did, one was always brought back the next day, and there were rooms on the ground floor with very beautifully forged ironwork on the windows and there one was lodged. I said that I would get out—in spite of everything.

In this institution they seemed to have a passion for cleanliness and fresh paint; on half the benches in the large park were signs saying "Fresh Paint." These signs were all elaborately painted as, one might say, with love, in a kind of monkish lettering, and in various colors. The small Gothic chapel, that had either sunk into the earth, or had been built with a cellar in mind at first and a church after, was also freshly painted. Among the stone arches that supported the roof there was a forget-me-not-blue sky with golden stars. The same blue paint was used on the cloak of the statue of the Virgin, and on it appeared those same somewhat shaky stars. The lettering under the tablets that showed the Stations of the Cross were done by the same hand and were like the sign at the end of the garden that said:

IT IS FORMALLY FORBIDDEN FOR
THE MESDEMOISELLES OF THE
CONVENT TO GO BEYOND THIS SIGN

It was in blue letters on a white background, and with four shaky golden stars in the four corners. The pole that held the sign was again lovingly painted in forget-me-not blue. All of this was done as if to apologize for the sternness of the message.

And there was the painter, on his knees, painting the windows of the boxes in which young vegetables are raised until they are set out. I went over to see him, and he had a long box with a handle and all his colors in this in pots, and when he looked up, he smiled. He had a long beard and I saw that it wasn't a painter, but an old priest. If he had been a painter I would have asked him why one could not go beyond that sign.

He smiled at me, got up with some effort, and made a sign with his hand to follow him. He walked a little distance to a hothouse that smelled of earth and empty flower-pots and flowers and plants. It was crammed with garden utensils, a wheelbarrow, hoses and shovels and the thousand and one things of the gardener, and it had a large table with many plants and a sink with water. Here he stopped and pointed, and to my great surprise I suddenly saw a large toad sitting under a fern. He hopped forward; he was like a piece of jewelry in several shades of gold and

precious stones—his immense mouth looked as if he had
something to complain about, and was in general unhappy
beyond any consolation. The priest took a small paint-
brush and brushed his head with it, and the toad closed
his eyes and swallowed with his whole underside which was
made of millions of small pearls, and he seemed to be very
happy. Then the priest let the water run, and with his
fingers put a few drops on the toad's head which also seemed
to give him pleasure. Then the priest smiled at me. There
was a large grindstone, with a foot pedal, and on another
table there were pruning knives and other instruments:
hedge clippers, and large shears taken apart to oil and
sharpen, scythes, and some carving knives.

I made my reverence to the priest, who went back to his
paintbox. I went back to the garden.

In the play period on the afternoon of the next day I
kicked a ball all the way back to the wall, at the end of the
forbidden piece of ground. When I came back, Veronique
stood breathless with the new friends, whose names were
Jacqueline and Racquel, and Veronique asked:

"What was back there?"

I told her that there was a barn, in the shape of a pagoda,
with hay in it, and then some dried wood to use in the
winter for fuel, and this dried wood was stacked like a wall,
between trees, and it led to the back of the main house
in which we lived. I thought that if one set fire to the barn,
the wind would come to one's aid and light the wood, and
the flames would soar up into the trees which were full
of autumn leaves all dry as paper, and from there it would
go to the roof of the place in which we slept, and the
convent would be on fire and we all would get out and be
sent home.

Was there no way out, I asked. No, said Jacqueline and Racquel. Back in that garden, farther back behind the pagoda, there was an opening in the wall, but it was nothing to get out through—only an elaborate oval-shaped hole in the wall with more heavy-forged grating and under it a brook. It was also impossible to get out through the water, for there were heavy iron staves, each one about a hand apart from the other, and also crisscrosssed the other way so as to form a grate. The trees there had large branches, but all those hanging out over the wall were cut away so as to make escape impossible.

"But why is this institution so tight and guarded?"

"Because during the war it was the headquarters of the German S.S. Nobody came in, and nobody got out, and in the vaults below they tortured their prisoners. You can go down there and see tables to which they tied them, and where they used irons to burn confessions out of them." Jacqueline would take us there. "Well then," I said to myself, "it will take the fire to get me out."

"Why can't one go back there then? If it's impossible to escape?"

"Because of the bad boys. There is a place where 'the worst element'—those are the words of the Mother Superior—assembles and they smoke, and call the young ladies of the institute our dear little virgin sisters, and then they use language quite unfit for the ears of little virgins, and they behave obscenely, making water—one of them is able to do it backward over his shoulder—saying dreadful words and throwing things, and the more one resents it the worse they behave. The leader of the gang, a boy whose name is Olivier, has a bicycle, and a shotgun, and the trees are filled with birds, and he is a good shot;

he takes aim, and bang—a little bird lies dead at your feet."

"So," said Racquel, "we don't go there, not on account of the sign, but because of the poor little birds that get killed."

I thought that I would put Monsieur Olivier in his place, and make him properly obedient to me.

The next day's playtime I went to the hothouse, and from the wall I selected the two pronged things that were used to trim hedges, and were as sharp as razors, a small ax, and some things which were stuck into the earth when planting. I took the smallest of these, and the ax, and practiced the way the Killer did. I was a little clumsy at first and then I got the feel of them.

Jacqueline was posted on guard, and on the third day I went back to the wall and the opening which I had studied, and there was Olivier, with his rifle, and he aimed into the tree and I said:

"Wait—unless you wish to lose your head."

He turned his head and he said:

"Watch this, little virgin sister—"

I let go with the small ax, and knocked the gun out of his hands.

He picked up his gun and called me a name. I answered him with soldier language and he was bewildered. The other ruffians moved closer to him, and I said, lifting one of the weapons:

"You, Olivier, stand here and face this gate, if you really have courage—and if you stand absolutely still—nothing will happen to you. But don't move or else an ear may come off."

So he shrugged his shoulder and smiled sheepishly, but he came forward and placed his face in the center of the ironwork, and I let go with two pruning knives—one to his right, one to his left—and they both sailed past him beautifully.

I said, "Pick them up and give them back to me."

He hesitated but when I lifted the third, the largest, he obeyed, and he brought them to the gate and he said:

"It's marvelous what you can do. What's your name?" I told him. He said, "I would like to see you again." The others crowded around, and they said, "We wish you could come out here and play with us." I said that I might, and that I would see them the next day at the same time, or else later if I could get out. But they were not to tell anyone. They promised. Olivier was their leader and strong and very handsome. I shook hands with all of them through the grating and I went back to the gardenhouse to put the tools back. I said good night to the toad, and then I went back to the playground.

The door was locked that night. And then I thought of tying bed sheets together and getting out through the window; three sheets or four would reach to the ground.

It was all now a question of good planning. The confederates outside the walls were ready to help us, once we were out. They knew a place where we could hide; they would hide us, and bring us food, and deliver the notes in which we would demand from our parents that we be given freedom at home—the condition upon which we would return. That would make the fire unnecessary.

It takes the child of a military man to think like that. I once overheard at home that it was written in the personnel dossier of Veronique's father, in the archives of the General Staff, that he was a good second in command, but no more. Papa said that he was sorry, but that Colonel de Voltera would always be a Colonel—and it showed in his daughter. Veronique could not make a plan, not to speak of putting it into execution; I had to drag her along. I had to go into her room and take the bed sheets off her bed, and bring them into mine. She was at the edge of tears.

I said, "This is how we knot them. Now we can't very well try the escape right off; we must first find out if the knot holds this way, or if we have to sew them together."

"Sew them together?" she bleated. "Where do we get needle and thread?"

That is what I mean—that kind of lack of resourcefulness. So we tied the first two sheets together, and I said:

"We'll test them for strength and length—the height to the third floor, plus our last body length. When we are hanging at the end, we can silently drop four feet more in our stockinged feet." The length was fine. Now we would test the strength.

We pushed the chair under the chandelier, and I got up and put the sheet over the two arms of the chandelier, first over one and then over the other so as to equalize the strain, and then I hung and said:

"Pull away the chair—you will see—" and at that moment there was white dust around me and a sudden descent and I sat on the floor. The chandelier had come down but swung close to the ground on the long wire that had followed it. There was a loud thump—and then all was still. I think that Veronique likes to be scared. She trembled all over, her eyes were dark holes in her head. She whispered in her crying voice in the darkness:

"Bon Dieu—what will happen to us now?"

I said, "Maybe they'll send us home—"

We opened the door and listened. The light at the end of the corridor was lit, but all was quiet; nobody came running. Maybe they thought that one of the girls had fallen out of her bed, or one of the Sisters. I said to Veronique that it was hopeless to try and fix the chandelier as it was very heavy. She was still shaking in her nightshirt, and I said, "Take your sheets, and go back and make your bed and go to sleep." So she did, and silently dragged the sheets out of the door and back into her room. I made my bed and fell asleep.

The descent of the chandelier was followed by the Conseil de Discipline the next afternoon, in the office of the Mother Superior.

We were playing on the tennis court, for here they had tennis balls and everything one could ask for, when Sister Marie Louise, who was known as "Sainte Nitouche," approached me. She was called by that name because she was very sweet and delicate, walked like a little doll, and carried her hands hanging from her wrists like wilted lilies, snow white and beautifully kept; one of these lilies came to life and pointed at me, and she said—as she said most things, with downcast eyes—that the Mother Superior wanted to see me. Now one goes with all the good wishes of one's friends, and the boundless joy of one's enemies, as if to an execution. There is a long corridor and then a heavy door, and a vestibule with a cocomat on which is written "Salve" and over this you walk and enter.

The Mother Superior is seated at her desk, and to the right and left sit all the Sister professors. Sainte Nitouche pointed to a spot in front of the desk and took her seat, and I looked at the Mother Superior and asked:

"What is wanted of me?"

The Mother Superior said: "First of all, it is wanted that you go out that door, and come in again, not barging into the room, but entering properly, like a young lady."

I asked: "How is properly?"

She said: "You come in and face me. You stop here, and you say 'Bonjour Madame.' Then you silently nod to each of the professors, looking at them from right to left. Then you remain silent and speak only when you are spoken to. And then you listen to what I have to say to you."

I went out and came in again as I had been told. Then the Mother Superior said:

"I have been told about the chandelier in your room. I suppose you know that it has been ripped down off the ceiling."

I said: "Oui, Madame. I did it."

She said: "Can you explain to us why? And how it happened?"

I said: "I told my mother not to send me here. I begged her not to. I told her that I would do anything to get out and run away from any institution she sent me to. She did not listen to me. She sent me anyway. I tried to get out the first night I was here but could not. My bed sheets were not long enough to reach to the ground from my window. Therefore I took Veronique's from her bed. I tied them and I wanted to try them out, and I used the chandelier, and it came down and that is all."

I expected that I would be sent home. But the Mother Superior, like everyone here, was filled with kindness. She looked at me very sadly and she said:

"My child, because this your first offense and because you have told the truth, there will be no punishment this time. Remain."

The professors agreed with this, and walked out. The Mother Superior told me to sit down, and she said that she knew how terrible these first days were, when one is away from one's parents, and away from home, and that she had a good deal of knowledge about young people, and that here she was like my mother, and that I could come to her at any time, with whatever troubled me.

"You will feel at home here, you will be happy with your fellow students, you will be one of our best pupils because you are an unusually intelligent girl and I have faith in you. I will not report this to your parents, and it will not be noted in your paper."

Then she recommended prayer to me and at last she said:

"For the time being, your bed will be placed in Veronique's room, until the damage is repaired, and then you will go back into your room. I don't want to lock you up, but you must promise me that you will not go out of the window. Will you promise me that?"

I said that I would not go out the window. I could promise that, for now there remained only the fire.

"We waited for you until late at night," said Olivier. I told him to send the others away.

I told him the story of the chandelier and I asked him to swear that what I would tell him would be secret. He spat on the ground and so did I, which sealed our lips. I said that the only way to get out was to set the place on fire and that I had someone who would help. Since all mail was censored he would have to mail a letter to Alain, to get him to come.

The gardener and the priest were in my room with two ladders, and they had hung the chandelier where it belonged. I wondered if le bon Père Sylvan would paint some crooked stars on my ceiling.

The next day I wrote the letter and Olivier came and got it; he secreted it in his blouse and swore to see that it was mailed.

11. THE FIRE

WHEN ONE WAITS for freedom, time passes with leaden steps. A letter from the convent to home would take a day, or two days; to get the answer another two days; that is four days. There were endless possibilities that it would be lost, or intercepted; perhaps Alain was ill in bed—and his mother would open it or, worse, his father. All this time there were lessons, and the days passed like a rock that you push up a hill. During the night it rolls back down on you.

Up at 6:00. At 6:30 morning gymnastics, after that Mass and Communion in the small chapel.

Classes at 8:00: French, mathematics, history, and religion. French as well as religion were given by Sainte Nitouche, because the old priest was too deaf and too old for religious instruction.

Lunch at noon.

Liberty until 2:00.

Then courses by choice in English, Greek, or Latin.

Classic dancing, by a teacher who came from outside the

gates, a properly accredited and stringy lady by the name of
Madame Tatiana.

From 4:00 to 5:00 an hour of liberty, which was the
time to see the bad boys; then an hour and a half of study
in the large hall. At 7:00 dinner, then half an hour of
liberty indoors. At 8:00 to the rooms, at 8:30 lights out.
In the morning and evening one had to reply to one's
name as it was read off by the Sister of the day.

I was interested in study, but could not keep my mind
on it. Sainte Nitouche tried to make her French classes
as interesting as possible:

> In 1839 being in great need of money, Honoré
> de Balzac decided to write a play, and he sent for four
> friends who were writers. Gautier arrived first and a
> servant led him to the place where Balzac was hid-
> ing.
> "There you are at last," cried Balzac. "I've been
> waiting for you for an hour. I am reading tomorrow
> for the theater manager Harel."
> "What are you going to read?"
> "A drama in five acts."
> "And you want my opinion?"
> "No—the play is not written yet."
> "Then it will be necessary to postpone the fire—
> for six weeks."

"Where does it say anything about fire?" asked Sainte
Nitouche. "Please pay attention— Now once more."
I excused myself and read:

> "Then it will be necessary to postpone the read-
> ing for six weeks."

"No," replied Balzac, "the play must be finished for tomorrow."

"Between now and tomorrow there is hardly time."

Sainte Nitouche complained again, "But what is the matter with you today. Please pay attention."

"No," replied Balzac, "the play must be finished for tomorrow."

"Between now and tomorrow, it is impossible. We should have hardly time to recopy it."

"The matter presents no difficulties—you will do one act, Ourliac another, Laurent Jan the third, Belloy the fourth, and I the fifth and I shall read the drama tomorrow at noon, as I promised."

"Tell me the subject, outline for me in a few words the characters," implored Gautier, "and I'll do my best."

"Ah, if it is necessary to tell you the subject," exclaimed Balzac, "we shall never get out of here."

"Please read that last line again."

"We shall never have finished."

This little needle of a woman, Sainte Nitouche, pointed at me, and asked what we had been reading. I stood up.

"About Honoré de Balzac, Madame."

"Correct, and what can you tell us about him?"

"That he always was in need of money, and that he never was discouraged about his enormous debts, and in order to be able to work without being disturbed by anyone he had various hidden dwellings, where neither his friends nor his creditors could find him. In these dwellings he worked all night, eating nothing, drinking only coffee."

"Very good."

I sat down.

I didn't eat anything either, and I worked all night thinking and planning. I prepared for the fire. I had discovered a way of getting out of the building at night. There was a circular stone staircase down the back of the building, and it led to the service part of the building. There was a window which could be opened noiselessly and outside of it was stacked some wood; and going out that way one could quickly gain the protection of the hothouse, and from there, under cover of the stacked wood, get to the pagoda and the wall.

Outside, in the daytime, I played around the escape window and arranged the wood there so that it was solid, and when I would finally climb out over it, the logs would not roll or fall and make a noise.

"There you are at last," I said like Balzac to Gautier when Alain arrived on the sixth day. He was on his bicycle, having ridden all the way, and I felt at once that now all would be well. His face was that of one who fights through all to victory—there was no doubt, no fear in it. He also had no unnecessary worries, or questions; merely when and how best to proceed. I felt that if he had wanted to he could have jumped over the high wall. What a difference there can be between children of the same parents.

When I told Veronique, she started to tremble. She clasped her hands and swallowed like the big toad, and put her hands to her throat.

I told her how it was all planned, and how we would be

free and back home in two days. The next morning she looked at me pleadingly. I said: "Remember you are with us, you are going to help." She looked like an old doll that a dog has played with for months. She nodded and said she would come along.

The time was set, and all had been prepared. Finally the night came.

At the end of dinner, as usual, we all went to our own rooms, and I waited in my bed in the long silence, counting every quarter hour until it would be midnight.

At the striking of quarter to twelve, I opened my door to go to Veronique's room. I went in my robe and in bare feet. She didn't answer my knocking; she had changed her mind and had locked her door. I couldn't make any noise, so I put on my dress and sneakers and went alone. I looked down the wide stairs and saw the Sister sitting there reading, and then I went down the kitchen stairs, out the window, over the stacked wood, and into the shadow of the trees. It was a warm and very clear night; it struck midnight and I ran so as not to be late for the rendezvous —and there was nobody there. I waited at the grated oval opening in the wall, looking out.

There was the village church, and the four steps that went along its façade sat silently in the moonlight, and I wondered if Alain too had become afraid. Then he came, and as he came closer I saw that it was Olivier. He carried a packet made of sackcloth, and in it were pieces of wood with more sackcloth wound around them and dipped into gasoline. Olivier said that he would hand them to me and then I would light them, but that he would not have anything to do with setting the fire; he did not have any matches. I was afraid it was all for nothing—when Alain came. He was breathless again, from bicycling, and excused himself for being late. He had matches, and he had a rope which he threw over the wall. I attached it to the iron grating, and in a moment he was over the wall and standing beside me. He gave me two of the torches, and he took two. He lit mine and his, and we flung them into the barn; then I saw him, lithe as a panther, go over the wall, and I went through the garden, without running, but looking back, and I carefully climbed back into the house, went to my room, and got into bed. I was very happy and satisfied with myself and with what I had done, and I waited. Again it took a long time.

Then all at once I heard the good Sisters, in their heavy boots, running and opening all the doors of our rooms, and saying:

"Don't be afraid—the barn is on fire but the fire will never get as far as this," and all the little sheeplike girls, half asleep, half terror-stricken, came "Baah, baah" crying out of their rooms.

Whenever something bad was done at home it was blamed on me and my brother Hugo and we were punished, guilty or not. And even if we were later found innocent, my father would say that it was good all the same, for it was punishment for something that had not been reported to him. This was a new experience—no one suspected, no one called for me. I stretched with pleasure—evildoing when done adroitly is very exciting. Nobody said, "You awful child, you have done this." That was the mood at the first moment of discovery of the fire.

Veronique came shaking and clung to me and said: "Oh, bon Dieu, if anyone finds out, what will happen to us?"

I said: "Why do you worry and tremble—you had noth-

ing to do with it; besides I will confess as soon as the
Mother Superior comes, and tell her I did it in order to
be sent home."

"But you will not be sent home," said Veronique. "The
police will come and you will go to prison—and then to
a reform school worse than anything here."

I said I would take a chance on that, and that I had told
my mother I would burn down the convent and so it was
her fault. Veronique cried, and said: "Please, please don't
tell for then I will be left here alone."

The Mother Superior came; she had a shawl over her
shoulders and she gave orders to take us down, out of the
building and out of danger. We dressed and went down,
and we saw the fire and the most wonderful sensations
filled me. I was elated. I stood there making the same face
as the others, looking at the fire, and I thought one thing
—they don't even know that it is beautiful. At last the fire
brigade came, and the water hoses played, and finally there
was a smell of smoke and burnt wood.

As the hour struck three the Mother Superior took us
all together to the chapel. There was the old deaf priest,
and the gardener, and everybody talked about the fire.
Veronique talked to me again, and she looked terrible. She
said:

"I implore you not to say you did it. Not only will you
be chased out of the church, and thrown in prison, and I
will remain here alone—but think of my poor brother.
The police will certainly find out that he was helping you
and my father will beat him half to death, and he will go
to prison, and his life will be ruined. It is bad enough if
they will find out by themselves—and I tremble when I

think of this—but please don't do anything to help them. Don't confess."

I don't like crying faces and pity and begging for mercy, but I felt that it would be terrible to hurt Alain, and I said to the sad face:

"Don't worry, no one will ever know. We will find another way out of this prison, but the next time you must promise not to quit."

"I swear," said Veronique.

Then one of the Sisters told us to be quiet, for the Mother Superior had something to say; then came the Mother Superior, and she walked directly toward me, and she looked very straight into my eyes. I said to myself, "Now you must forget that you did this, and put it out of your mind," so that I could look at her very calmly and innocently. She asked me nothing and I said to myself that it would be very easy to kill someone and never be caught as the murderer.

The Mother Superior said that by the grace of the good Lord we had all been saved, and to say a prayer of thanks, and then we would get a glass of warm milk and go back to bed.

And then the Mother Superior smiled at us out of her strong face and stood with her hands in the sleeves of her habit while we passed by and said, "Good night, Madame."

12. MADEMOISELLE DURANT

THE TIME in which one absorbs the new passed. We were used to the sound of the church bells, to the faces and names of the nuns, to our seats at table and pews in chapel. I always felt a pain in my heart in the vegetable garden, for it reminded me of home. We were also used to the steps everywhere and now could run up and down them without counting them. This side of the house was higher than the other, and a ball rolled by itself. In the hothouse, besides the toad, there was a pet lizard. The old gardener was our friend. The studies were terribly hard, the hours long. The old priest was our Father Confessor. He was very kind and as deaf as Auguste the chauffeur at home, and one could confess the most terrible things to him and he gave the same penitence for setting the convent on fire as for taking the name of the Lord in vain. All this time nothing happened. I plotted several escapes, all in vain. Finally a new pensionnaire arrived. It was just before lunch. We heard two bells ringing, one at the gatehouse announcing an arrival, and one for lunch. We all ran down to the door and we saw coming toward the house, in a cloud of dust between the rows of poplars, a black Cadillac with a uniformed chauffeur. It stopped where we were standing.

We stopped talking. The chauffeur got out of the car, opened the door of the limousine, cap in hand, and a girl, very beautiful and blond, came out of the car. She had her eyes lowered, and without looking at anybody she mounted the steps to the terrace, like someone walking in a dream. I stood there, and slowly advanced one foot so that she would trip over it, and fall flat on her face on the stone. But she still had her eyes lowered, and she saw my foot. She looked up at me. I was the first person she saw and we were enemies from that moment on.

I said to myself, this will be my victim until the last day we are together.

She went inside, and the girls had their mouths open because here came the second stupefaction: the chauffeur took seven matching valises from the baggage compartment of the large car. Our dear old gardener, Gustave, whom I loved dearly, had to carry them all inside. But this was not the end of surprises, for now, out of the other side of the Cadillac, came what looked like a governess, but turned out to be a maid.

The Sisters and the Mother Superior suffered from snobbism, and not so much of adoration of names or titles as of money which of course served their interest. If we arrived with our parents, with one valise, a Sister showed us to our room. We were immediately clothed in the uniform which had been designed by a great couturier, made to our measure, and sent on ahead of time. If we arrived at nine, we did immediately whatever was done at nine, if at noon we went to lunch. Mademoiselle Gladys Durant, however, upset the entire routine. The Mother Superior received her with two Sisters at her side, and they went up to her room; we all were fascinated by this reception. The ones among us who had no imagination, the poor girls who would grow up to be good little women and mamans were all aglow, and they effused to each other: "Oh, Albertine, Martine, Jacqueline—isn't this like a fairy tale—she looks like a beautiful puppet and what parents she must have to give her all that and let her have a permanent hair-do and painted fingernails."

Lunch was delayed; then finally it was ready and we were all seated. Nobody ate because all awaited the arrival of Mademoiselle Durant in the dining hall.

There were maids to serve at table, all in black with white aprons and a white bonnet on their hair. They were not of the Order but civilians—they also waited. There was a kind of omelette rolled up and inside it champignons and cut-up ham and chicken; it was a good dish, but had to be served and eaten quickly as it got soggy. The platters were standing on the serving table, the cook was complaining, and finally Mademoiselle entered, still with two Sisters. She had changed. She was in a new and lovely dress, not yet in the uniform of the institution. The tables were placed, one here—one there, irregularly, and there were flowers on them, and winding through these tables came the Mother Superior, then Mademoiselle Durant, then the other two Sisters, and then the rest of the staff of the institution. We were all eager to see where she would sit— and, hélas, the Mère Superieure advanced to my table, took both hands from inside her large sleeves, and pointing at the chair next to me with one hand and at me with the

other, introduced us and placed Gladys with me. One of
the Sisters pulled back her chair and the Mother Superior
said to me, smiling: "Be kind to her, she is new, and one
must always be especially nice to the new ones." And standing up, since I was being addressed by the Mother Superior,
I said:

"You may have confidence in me, my Mother."

The new arrival sat down, and the service began very
quickly, the servants stumbling about with the omelettes. I
said to the new one, pushing my plate away, and refusing
the omelette—

"Let me tell you, you have come to an awful place! As
a friend, be advised—look at me. Since I came here I have
turned yellow and lost weight. I am down to seventy pounds
—the food is awful, last week two girls were almost poi-
soned. There is bread that you needn't be afraid of unless
you break it open and find a cockroach baked inside, but
all else—beware of."

The servant girl came to our table with the omelette
and Mademoiselle Gladys had also pushed her plate aside,
and said:

"No, thank you. I think it is the voyage that has upset
me."

She ate nothing. Then came the rest period. What was
very amusing now was how the various sections of the institution divided themselves. There were a few like Gladys,
who were daughters of the bourgeoisie—of Lyon, of Mar-
seille, of Paris—who sought to start a friendship, and smiled
at Gladys; and there were we, in the minority, who stood off.
We met in our observatory, the place where we could observe anyone coming, at the head of the stairs, with plaster
angels and rococo décor. We sat there, each one with her

back against one of the four pillars so that we could see anyone coming up the stairs or down the corridors, and we plotted.

One of the girls of our group said:

"Why don't we try and be nice to her, she may change this place for the better, for she has privileges and they will have to give us the same, or nearly the same, and we may also get things from her."

I said: "No—I know exactly what she is and what she stands for."

That evening, I didn't eat anything again, and I got her to say to the servant in her shrill voice—when the dish was passed—"No, thank you. I am not used to this kind of food." This was a major offense, nobody ever said that— and we thought she would be sent from the table; but again the incredible happened. The Sister in charge of the dining room came and asked if Mademoiselle had any special wishes, and wanted a substitute—so they brought her a plain omelette. She took a forkful and looked at me— what to do?—and I looked back at her with such disgust that she put the fork back and pushed the plate away.

She said: "You are right—the food is uneatable. Yes, and all the money our parents have to pay to have us here."

I looked at her and said:

"You can help us a great deal—for evidently you are of importance, and I don't know what your father has done for this pensionnat—or for the Order—but you are in a position to change things and one must be radical. Gladys, take the plate with the awful omelette that is uneatable and throw it on the floor."

Gladys took the plate, and with an expression of outrage, threw it on the floor—spattering the omelette. Normally, when something like this happened, the Sister said: "Go to your room."

The Mother Superior was called. She saw the serving woman on the floor cleaning up, and when the story had been told to her, she looked at me for a long time and then placed Gladys at another table. Now the Mother Superior had placed her at the table of the biggest nouveau riche. We sat up in the corridor and plotted what would come next, for now that she had encountered girls of her class she turned and showed her real colors. She had a vicious and vulgar character—it displayed itself in a thousand details; she cut us.

Our next encounter was in the chapel. It was on Sunday; we were in our uniforms, Gladys in a lovely dress. She passed before me and there flowed from her a cloud of heavy and very expensive perfume. I called a Sister and I asked if I might leave the chapel, for I felt unwell.

I sat outside on the stairs—and there Gladys passed me after chapel. I stopped her, and said to her:

"Listen you. I hate this uniform we are wearing, and there are here the daughters of marquises, dukes, and counts, and we all have to wear it—and we all have one valise like in a prison—and there are no exceptions. If tomorrow you are not changed to be like us something very unpleasant will happen to you."

She said: "I have the right to dress exactly as I please, but if it makes you happy, someday, when I feel like it, I may wear the uniform."

I said: "Oh no, you will wear it from now on."

I went to the big house, to the sewing room where the scissors were kept, and then I went to Gladys' room and started to cut up her dresses. A door opened and one of the Sisters entered, and she took me down to the Mother Superior, who looked at me and said: "My child, I don't understand you at all—you are so good and you are so bad —and both these qualities fight in you and all your life you will be persecuted by yourself. I feel very sorry for you." She tried to put her arms around me, but I shrank and put my shoulders together. I cannot stand acts of forgiveness or tolerance, motherly kisses or kindness; I am used to punishment.

The bill for the dresses was sent to my parents. I was denied all privileges for two weeks, but I had the satisfaction of seeing Mademoiselle Durant in uniform the same day. She looked well in hers.

13. LE PÈRE FRAMBOISE

As in a prison, arrivals and departures were the only form of excitement here. One day the bell rang again, and the new chaplain arrived in a taxi, with a very smart new traveling bag, held together by a leather strap. The convent shutters were shaken by horrible assaults of the wind, dark gray and blue clouds passed over the roofs, and leaves began to fall.

The mood in the convent was as triste as that of nature. For the beloved Père Sylvan was to be replaced. Père Sylvan and his sacristan, the old gardener, had been at the convent longer than anyone else, and they were part of it. The old priest was like le bon Père at Beaufort, again the good Lord walking the earth.

He was like one of the polychrome saints in his chapel. Sometimes he slept in the sun and his eyes were shut hard, so that one thought it would take an oysterman's knife to open them. When they opened, then there appeared the two little black peppercorns of his pupils—the sharp look of the deaf who hear with their eyes.

He stood here and there, always lovely to look at and serene—combing his white Father Christmas beard with a huge iron comb, or else he was in the flower garden, or in the hothouse with his toad, or feeding the carp. Mostly he wandered about with the gardener, who carried the long wooden box with the paints, and they touched up things that needed it, made signs, or painted garden benches and tables. They were in harmony with themselves and all about them.

He was also interested in fishes. There was a small round pool, with a mound of rocks in the center and a small statue of the Virgin; in this, among algae and water plants, were some half-dozen fat carp, who all came to the edge of the pool when they saw the old priest, put their heads out of the water saying O—O—O silently, and then slid back under, gulping and disturbing the water, and stayed there as he fed them. He cried out loudly that in a few days it might freeze and, since he would not be here any more to look after them, his friends would come to a bad end. He told each one of us everything, in the manner of the very old, repeating it really to himself. He said these poor people would starve to death, for nobody would remember to feed them through the ice and snow all winter long. The old gardener brought a net and also a large dish in which one might have cooked them, and we watched him catch the carp which then were carefully carried to the brook that ran through the property and whose water was in motion and did not freeze. But the last one of the fat fishes hid in the greenery near the center.

The gardener was told to bring a large ladder, which he placed across the pool, and Father Sylvan, who was agile for his age, rolled up his sleeves, and lay on the ladder over the water, and talking to the carp he said, "Come—let me help you, it's better for you that way." The carp kept saying silently O—O—O, made several turns, lay sideways, looked up, and then swam toward le bon Père, and almost into his hands as if he understood. The priest lifted him from the pond with ease and placed him in the large basin in which the gardener carried him to the brook.

These were sad days, and the Mother Superior was almost always alongside the good Father Sylvan, sitting beside him on benches, and when he didn't sleep, they talked. They talked the sad talk that has to be, after it has been delayed to the ultimate moment; this dreadful business of the end of life and the waiting for the entrance to Paradise to which all knew he would go, and probably very soon. For having spent all his life as a priest in the region, and forty years at the convent, he would certainly, after being torn out by the roots by his own will, soon pass on. With the acceptance of things ordained, he sat like one condemned.

The Mother Superior had exhausted every effort to have him stay on but he was simply too old and had to be replaced.

There was then the problem of how to ease him out without unnecessary heartaches, and how to install the new priest.

It was decided that Father Sylvan would stay on awhile, until the younger man became familiar with the routine of the convent. He would then read an early Mass, after which he would remain in his comfortable quarters and it would all take place on that day, the thought of which made

every one of the Sisters weep. They prayed daily and implored heaven that a miracle produce itself, for they loved
him as if he were their father, and also their baby. They
cooked for him, looked after him when he was ill, watched
his flowers grow, and made jams of the fruit he raised.

He was a vegetarian and loved salads, and he even apologized for that, for he said that carrots and celery and salad
leaves really belonged to the rabbits.

One day Sister Marie Thérèse came into class, hardly
able to speak, and with her mouth trembling, said that the
new chaplain, Père Ambroise, was expected presently. She
broke into sobs after this and most of the girls also cried—
and then all the other Sisters went about dabbing at their
eyes, and the whole convent was red-eyed, and everybody
knew that no matter how good the new priest, a bon Père
Sylvan he would not be.

After he arrived, we looked out of the windows; we
watched him walk. He was tall and thin, very good-looking
and with sharp features, and all the girls said, "Oh, regardez
comme il est beau." He was even more attractive when we
were presented to him. It happened at the hour of Cate-
chism. Every one of the pensionnaires stood up before him
as the Mother Superior said the names, Mademoiselle so
and so, on through the class of twenty-two girls. He was
very distant and afraid to look at us; he inclined himself
and gave a kind of silent benediction. He was very elegant
and he had a complexion like a young girl, very large blue
eyes and blond hair, brushed or rather cut like an ample
crew cut, and a long thin neck. Now seeing him inside very
close, he was all and more than he had seemed to be outside. Very tall, very elegant, very thin, much too good-
looking for a priest.

Veronique said: "He is out of a good stable—" an expression her father used in describing someone very comme il faut.

He was obviously from the best of families. There were small accents about him that also spoke of riches. His soutane was as if from Dior: the best cloth, and all sewn by hand, and fitting perfectly. The neat collar sat right, snow-white and hard, and around it the black which is open in front about two inches wide and with rounded edges. Then the long row of black buttons down the front, and between the third and fourth of these, there was clamped a golden fountain pen, diagonally, the cap outside, the rest inside the cloth. This was very chic we thought. Then on his hip over the hipbone, where the long flaring skirt of the soutane started, he had a small watch pocket and a gold chain again disappearing inside of him. The wide sash around his middle that hung down the side was meticulously cut and adjusted. His shoes were cared for and of the best leather and cut. Mostly he stood ramrod straight —and in back of his soutane he had two pockets, and since he had no buttocks, but a straight drop there, he sometimes put both his hands into these pockets, with only the neat starched cuffs showing; and he stood aloof in this his favorite pose, compelling us to admire him—as most French youths do, collecting this tribute from the drab females as their proper due. I thought how Papa would approve of him. This was the material for a chaplain for his collection of the ideal soldiers.

He stood close to the window in his favorite pose or walked with his sash flying—he did not fit into the convent. He had arrogance in his mien, and while he was shy, he seemed to say in his motions and voice: "Just wait until I have you under my control and then—" He reminded me of Don Felice. His look burned at times. At the sides of his lips were two thin hard lines which became pronounced when he smiled, but he smiled very seldom—only when he bowed to the Sisters on entering and leaving. He also assumed an air of absolute authority over them—a waiting air. I was seated at the first desk in order that I could always be under surveillance. He sailed past this in long strides back and forth several times. He blushed very easily and on the third day we had changed his name from Père Ambroise to Père Framboise on account of the sudden flushes that appeared on his cheeks.

He led in prayer. He liked to draw on the blackboard with white chalk, illustrating various religious subjects, but always turned quickly so as not to let us out of his sight. When he caught someone making faces, his eyes flashed, he blushed, and one heard the swish of a whip although he had none in his hand. He was a punisher. He usually stopped at my desk, and rested his long, very well manicured hands on it. He called on me frequently, but did not like my answers. I have a retentive memory, and practically threw answers at him, like pawns in a game of no particular value. That brought blushes; he would rather have liked to have me stammer or not know. It was a play for position. He looked at me with inquiry then, sometimes benign, kind, and occasionally improperly—or else he did not know the language of the eyes. I knew that here was another who would try and subjugate me. The game was on—how early one knows this, or else never. It depends on how you are made. I did not let him out of my sight as I stood there, in the first line. The lesson started. He asked many questions, and I kept my eyes on him; when he spoke, he used a set of hand motions, a little theatrical, and after he had spoken a few words he always cleared his throat and looked down or reached up at his collar—all to hide his nervousness. He had a very good voice, and when he spoke on morality and religion it was as if a poet complained of the conditions on earth rather than a preacher who accused. He always said softly: "You understand, my children, we are in this world to love, to give." At first he said this always looking at me softly. Later he found a way of placing his hand on my head and then on my shoulders, with his finger tips feeling their way toward my neck; he had very long tapered fingers. I hate to be touched. "Vous comprenez mes enfants, nous sommes sur cette terre pour aimer et nous donner"—and I said to myself, "Just wait—I will give you something to remember me by, Father Framboise." And every morning when I entered class and he came and greeted me with a special look of silent sympathy, I smiled and I said to myself with pity for him, "Mon vieux, you don't know what's awaiting you." But I did not know as yet what I would do; it was like having a rabbit on the table, and a knife and also the casserole and thinking of how to cook him. The weak soft look of love in his eyes grew, and I was trying to find the solution to the problem of how to cook him.

I said one day to Veronique, as we took our daily walk in the autumn winds, pushing our feet through the yellow foliage of the poplars on the way down to the gate, "I think I have found a way of getting us both out of this sacred convent school. You remember the promise you gave me to help the next time I needed you?" She said she did and that this time I could count on her. I told her it wouldn't be anything like setting the convent on fire, but that the good

Père Framboise would help us to get out and that we would not have to wait long for the opportunity.

It offered itself soon. One day at six in the morning I called Veronique, who knew how to whistle very well, which I could not do yet—she whistled strong and like a boy. I took her to the window of my room. Outside the window were the autumn brown branches of an old, heavy walnut tree. I pointed down. Around the trunk of the tree ran a bench, and on this sat le Père Framboise—reading his breviary and looking up between pauses to my room. Outside of my room was a small balcony and the windows were really French doors that opened all the way to the bottom. I said to Veronique: "I will give you the signal when to whistle." I opened both doors wide, as wide as possible. I took off my pajamas and giving Veronique the signal stepped out on the balcony. The blue eyes of the young priest searched the façade of the house for a moment, and when he saw me standing on the balcony absolutely nude he rose, blushed, dropped his breviary, and he cried: "Mon enfant! Mon enfant!" and I cried as if being surprised: "Mon Père! Mon Père!" I went back into the room quickly and closed the door and the curtains.

In class that day he did not look at me, nor did he touch the subject of love or giving, nor put his hand on my head or shoulder. I kept looking at him as if nothing had happened.

"Now tomorrow," I said to Veronique, "we must do the same thing, but not at six, for at six he will expect this again, and we have to make him uncertain, so we will do it at five minutes after six." We waited for the bell in the church steeple to toll six, and then watched the tree. We were right. He was there at six reading in his breviary, and as we watched him through the curtains we saw how occasionally he gave a quick glance upward. At five after six Veronique repeated the whistle and the opening of the window, and I stepped out nude. He rose like a frightened horse, and cried: "Mais, mon enfant, qu'est-ce que vous faites encore!" Then he said: "Will you go inside instantly."

"Mais oui, mon Père," I said, and going inside closed the window. Veronique, who had watched all this lying prone on the carpet, got up and asked, what were we going to do next? So came the morning of the third day.

On French windows there are fixtures which are called "Persians"; they are like Venetian blinds but are made of metal and fold sideways like a screen. I usually slept with them open, but this night I closed the windows, and also the Persians, giving an air of having shut myself completely in—for it usually takes a servant to open them. They have very strong hinges and the part where they go together is hard to secure. Now it was six again, and through the Persians we could look down and we saw him there, reading in his breviary and looking up. I gave the signal to Veronique. She whistled, I kicked open the Persians and was out at the balcony nude. The time was six-ten, and, as in a theater, everything was timed—but the surprise was that the Mother Superior suddenly appeared from behind the walnut tree. Le Père Framboise said nothing, again blushing. He looked at the Mother Superior and pointed to my window. She looked up as if she saw the Devil. We closed the shutters. The young priest left, saying to the Mother Superior that he wanted to see me after Mass. We went to Mass every day at seven.

In the sacristy after Mass, Père Framboise, blushing again, pointed to a prie-dieu. "Kneel down, my child," he

said, "and go into yourself for awhile. You have need of it."
I was still on my knees before him, when he asked:

"Why do you do that?"

I couldn't stand it any more. I burst out laughing and said:

"Pour vous faire plaisir, mon Père."

Now he had a little disappointed baby mouth and that got very angry, as if he were about to cry. He was not made for anything sinister. Since his face failed him—and his pale eyes said nothing—he raised his arms, also in a futile gesture. He said, overloud and not in control of his voice:

"But you do not know what you are doing to me! What you have been doing all along! I am a priest," he said, "not an ordinary man." He stamped his foot and said:

"And I have seen nothing." He paused and then he said:

"But tell me—if an ordinary man, not a priest had passed by, would you have done the same thing?"

I said: "A man dressed like a priest, or a man dressed in any other fashion is always a man."

"Non non, mon enfant," he said, blushing anew and deeper than usual. "You will understand later."

"Yes yes," I said to myself, "and you also will understand."

He told me to get up, gave me his benediction, and told me to go.

"What now?" asked Veronique.

"Now we wait," I said.

The Mother Superior called me into her room and she said, with shame in telling me and never looking at me, that never in her life had she had to do with anything like this, and she asked:

"Why did you do that?"

I said: "Ma Mère, I have no explanation. But when I see that it is six—and I know he waits for that moment as I do—and I know he is down below—I have an uncontrollable desire to show myself nude."

"Promise me," said the Mother Superior, "that you will never do this again."

I promised; I always keep my promise no matter to whom given. In this case it was easy to promise, for I knew there was no need to do it again.

Three days passed without anything happening on either side. Only now the old gardener passed below at six, evidently posted by the Mother Superior, and busied himself raking the leaves that fell out of the autumn-burned walnut tree. Dear old Gustave raked there faithfully until it was time for church.

On the fourth day, as always, I awoke before six. The birds were singing, the gardener raking. I was sitting in bed brushing my hair—the curtains were drawn, the Persians folded—when there was a soft knock at my door. I said, "Enter," knowing who it would be—and it was le Père Framboise. He closed the door in back of him, very quietly, and he said, with his voice held low and his blue eyes large and shining:

"I am happy that you have obeyed, my child." He sat down on a chair, folded his hands, and looked at me.

I said: "Mon Père, you know you do not have the right to enter any of these rooms."

He answered: "A priest has the right to enter into any place, as long as he comes to do good."

He started to talk about what good I had done. He said that he thought of what had happened as having no importance because it was an act of youthfulness, and that I had no conception of its gravity. But such things lead to worse things—and with that he moved from the chair to the bed. He spoke as one who wants to embalm another in words. He did exactly what I expected; he placed his hand on my leg. I sat up. I was wearing pajamas—I crossed my legs like a tailor. He leaned over me, took me by the shoulders, and started to kiss me.

I cried: "Veronique! Veronique!"

Veronique had been properly instructed in her role and told what to do if I cried out her name. She did not fail me this time, she was vive, and locked the door to my room from the outside. She ran down to get the Mother Superior, and in a minute all the girls, the Sisters, and the Mother Superior were in the corridor—the little lambs all trembling.

Le Père Framboise was redder than he had ever been and he seemed unable to move; he did not try to save himself. The Mother Superior came in and shielded me with her large figure, and she told the Sisters to get the little ones out of the room. She told the Père Framboise to get out immediately and she said to me to be calm, and called me a "poor child." I was pardoned, but we did not see the Père Framboise again; he was sent away that day. But as for getting out of the convent—I had failed again. In fact I had done a good deed. The Mother Superior looked pleased with me, arranged my cravat when I passed her, and said to me that I was a very good pupil—my marks had improved—and that those who give trouble sometimes end up the very best.

Then she looked deep into me with her clear eyes and she said: "I pray that one day, the obligatory obstinacy of your nature will turn for your good, that you will allow

yourself to be kind—to love someone beside yourself—
and then you will be happy." She kissed me on the forehead.

Le bon Père Sylvan was reinstated. He read the Mass at
seven-thirty again, listened to the confessions, fed worms
to his toad, and slept his sleep here and there, sometimes
looking like a gray mossy statue.

Innocent of the affair of the window, although everyone
told him in confession, he preached in his beautiful Gothic
chapel the next Sunday and looking up to heaven, he said
that the ways of the Lord were at once mysterious and
wonderful.

14. GLADYS IN COLOR

MADEMOISELLE GLADYS DURANT was always in proper uniform now and ate quietly at table. Some disliked her less than others but everyone was sickened by the privileges still extended to her, especially the one concerning written lessons. These had to be handed in at a specific time, and if they were not, then whoever was late received a zero. That is, all except Gladys. One day we noticed that both Veronique and I received zeros, which we could not afford, and Gladys received none. All this was bad enough but worse and insufferable was her attitude of letting us know that she was privileged and had no need to worry. We decided to do something about it.

We went up to the observatory and sat with our backs against the pillars and thought about what we could do. Something had to be done, for the smug smile with which she had the habit of passing us was too much.

Since the successful coup with le Père Framboise, there had taken place a change in Veronique. She was less the shaky carcass now. She said to me: "I want to be like you—

I admire you immensely," and then she embraced me.
Scenes like this make me cringe. But I put her back in her
place by saying that she was quite acceptable as she was,
and that nobody should try to be anything but themselves.
To thine own self be true was a very important statement.
So she said that she was more herself now than she had
been, and that I could count on her. What could we do to
Gladys to get her off her high horse? I promised I would
think about what we could do short of actually killing her.

We were walking around the grounds, thinking, and we
visited the hothouse and the toad, and stroked his head;
and I saw the box with the colors. Then we passed by the
administration building, and saw that one of the maids was
going into the infirmary. This maid, Louise, was very nice
and our friend, and we stopped to speak to her. She had a
little bottle, and she said she was going to get some ether
from the infirmary, for Mademoiselle Gladys had soiled one
of her uniforms and had asked her to remove the spot. We
went back into the big house and up to the observatory.
For a week we worried about what to do to teach her a
lesson, and then I found a way of scaring her to death.

I went into her room as the bells rang midnight, and sat
on her bed. She slept peacefully like a doll. On her bedside
table was a golden hand mirror, and a brush and comb to
match. I pressed slightly on her arm.

Suddenly, and with a yell, she sat up in bed. I said:

"You are the most ignoble being in school and we have
decided to get rid of you. We have found a way of killing
you which harmonizes well with your personality, with the
many lovely colors about you, with the beauty of your
hair, and nails, and blue slippers—and golden comb and
brush." She turned on the light. She sat up as I talked and

I saw that she slept in her skin, which was against the rules of the pensionnat. She took the mirror in the golden frame, combed her hair, and said to me:

"Go back to your room or I will call for a Sister. You are mad."

I said: "You just wait and see what happens to you, and you can call and call, and no one will be able to come to help you."

Next night at midnight, I told her: "The way of killing you we have discovered comes from experiments made with a liquid. It has the characteristic of killing you by leaving you like a rainbow or a fireworks display, aglow, in all colors." To make somebody really scared you have to tell them very little at a time—and let them worry.

At last the next night she sat there scared. So now the moment had come. I said to Veronique:

"Tomorrow, you get the sponge and the ether." And in the gardener's hothouse there was the box with the paints that he used: red, brown, heavenly blue, green and yellow, and gold. It had a handle and brushes for the various colors.

We got the ether and cotton from the infirmary. We carried the box with the colors up the stairs, and at three everything was ready. We put the ether on a pad of cotton and then we decided we would go in very quietly and both jump at her, Veronique holding her while I applied the sponge. We carried our box with colors to the door and at the stroke of twelve we went in. Gladys was asleep—and one, two, three, we had her.

She opened her eyes and struggled and tried to scream, but in this effort she drew in ether and in a few moments she was limp. Now we took the sheet off. She lay there motionless. Dipping the heavy brushes we painted her as though painting a house; one leg blue, one arm red and white, one arm green. The face we made all red and that went well with the blond hair. The effect was tremendous. We turned her around and Veronique whistled while we did this, and here and there we put an extra splotch. Her bottom we painted golden, and the bottom of her feet we painted one black, the other brown. We were working fast. When she was finished we were very satisfied, because we had been afraid that it would not go so well. We embraced each other. We took the colors back to the hothouse and put the cotton into the toilet. When we went to bed it was five o'clock.

In the morning, on the way to the chapel at seven, a Sister always read off the names. When Sainte Nitouche, who was the Sister of the day, came to Gladys' name and there was no answer, Sainte Nitouche asked:

"Has anybody seen Mademoiselle Gladys?"

Since our rooms were next to hers she asked Veronique and me whether we had seen Gladys. Shaking our heads we said we had not seen her, so the Sister said:

"Perhaps she is sick—"

She asked one of the girls to go to her room. We waited and then we heard frightful screams from upstairs, and the girl that had been sent cried from the window of Gladys' room:

"Ma Soeur, ma Soeur, Gladys is dead. She is dead in colors!" she cried.

So Sainte Nitouche ran and everybody after her. We also ran to see what had happened to Gladys.

When Sainte Nitouche saw Gladys, she lost her head completely. She said to the children, "Don't enter—this is too terrible," and she closed the door behind her and ran for the Mother Superior. Two other Sisters came, and then one at the head, one at the feet, they carried Gladys in a sheet out of her room, and the green arm was hanging out on one side, and the zebra-striped on the other, and two girls fainted, and one of the Sisters said:

"I have never seen anything like it, how can a girl's face turn a color like this?"

For two hours and a half they scrubbed her with soap and with alcohol. She awoke around eight, and when she saw herself, she fell back into unconsciousness, and then she awoke again at nine and cried, and then she told the Mother Superior that I had visited her for a week and threatened to kill her.

The Mother Superior called for me and she said that she could no longer keep me, and that I would have to leave the convent. She informed my parents I had to pack and leave in an hour. The Mother Superior said:

"It is clear that you could not do this alone—no use telling me who it is—I know."

I saw the old gardener on the way out. He had a bouquet of flowers which he handed to me, and the old priest said:

"In this garden are many wild flowers, but you are the wildest of them," and he kissed me and gave me his blessing and I said good-by.

I packed twice that day, for my father had covered himself with glory. He had been appointed to command the troops of occupation in Germany. And that is where we went. My parents did not mention anything about what had happened in school. My only consolation was that Veronique was thrown out as well; her father was a Colonel also and she too went to Germany with her parents and her brother Alain.

PART TWO

1. HOHENLINDEN

WE MOVED INTO A HOTEL in Weimarein, and although we occupied a whole floor Papa was extremely irritated that his bathroom was not right and that he was too confined. The Killer bore the brunt of his bad humor. The mood improved somewhat when the expected announcement of his promotion to the rank of General came. He would be in charge of the Occupation forces around Weimarein and we would move into the castle of a wine baron, located on a hill overlooking the city.

The brother of the man who had owned the castle, a German ex-General by the name of Count Werner von der Linde, presented himself and immediately endeared himself to Papa by addressing him as General and Your Excellency, and also Herr General. He was a very unprepossessing man, whether on account of being out of uniform and in the state of demoralization of all Germans of this time or whether on account of his nature. He was neat, small, and, except for a certain stiffness of bearing, looked more like a philosopher or mathematics professor than a general.

He sucked in air when he spoke, and on his nervous face there played a constant obliging smile; it laid bare his teeth, as if the lips had been cut away and the mouth opened. He wore a monocle. He had short-cut gray hair, a very hard look, green, the color of a Moselle bottle; he was forever aware, he seemed to have a heavily charged conscience. He also seemed like someone who has to talk to somebody or else go mad.

Papa received him with the respect that the aristocrat and General would extend to his equal and colleague. General von der Linde gratefully accepted a cigarette which Papa lit for him, drank a whisky, and said that when convenient to Papa the castle, named Hohenlinden, could be visited and arrangements made to take over.

Papa said he was ready now, and they left together and drove up the mountain road. Papa came back elated. There was everything he expected. It was an immense property compared to which the castle at Beaufort was a doll's house.

The Killer could imitate people, and picked up words like a parrot. We had a special language among us which the Killer adopted, and which is the language of young people of our kind in France. The word "terrible"—pronounced with a long *i* like "terriiible"—means something very good and very beautiful: a terrible car is a very fast sports car, a terrible picture or record is an exceptional film or dance tune.

When something is even greater than terrible, then it is "vachement" something—"vache" is cow, and is usually a derogatory term. A policeman is a "vache"—my father was called "peau de vache"—but in the same sense as the word "merde" is employed in France both to condemn and praise—for example "Oh merde" is said when you hit your finger with a hammer or some other small disaster befalls you; "merde alors" is used in admiration of a beautiful painting, or anything that astonishes you with its appeal and perfection from a sporting event to art—"vachement beau" is the highest praise one can give a person. "Cowlike beautiful" is like out of this world—incredible—the maximum. A girl or a boy can be "vachement beau." Then there are things that are sensational; in this case, the word "sensational," being too long, is cut down to "vachement sensas": the "sensas" is given a deep broad *a*—"vachement sensaaas." A party can be "vachement sensas," a person can be "vachement sympat"—again a deep long *a*: in this case the word "sympathetic" has been trimmed. Something can also be "vachement trance," which is vachement entrancing.

"How is it really?" we asked the Killer when he got back. "Terriiible! Vachement sensaaas—vachement trance," he said. "Unimaginable."

He had never dreamed anything like it existed. The most formidable feature of the castle proper was in the basement, if one could call it that, for it was like the cellars of the Louvre or the corridors of the Paris Métro, and here, through heavy doors, one entered a vast gallery with a bank of elevators.

The mountain was like a coal mine—seventeen miles of shafts and tunnels, with wine-tasting rooms on every level all elaborately furnished; electric trolleys the length of the shafts, a railroad siding at the lowest level, millions of bottles of wine on racks. There was the castle itself with terraces, stables, garages, tennis courts, and indoor and outdoor swimming pools—all of it "terriiible."

Papa arranged to have his belongings moved up immediately. His bathroom now was "vachement trance," with a sunken tub, or rather a small mosaic pool in which he could really play like a seal and do his exercises. He gave orders that General von der Linde was to be properly saluted and he invited the old gentleman to come whenever he wanted to. He had discovered that General von der Linde was a member of the German society of tin soldiers. The Killer said that it did not matter what nationality they were, generals were all the same, skins of cows—but that ours at least was a centaur and the real thing, and a winning one. He said that von der Linde had remarked that there was only one thing more demoralizing than being a general who had lost his army, and that was being an admiral who was retired. "Imagine," he said, "not to have all that glory, suddenly, overnight—to lose your battleships and the oceans with it."

There was another bond between the Generals—they were both Napoleon-crazy, true Bonapartists. In one of the salons of Höhenlinden was a bust of Napoleon. Papa had almost clicked to attention when he came upon it. They were in such accord that in one of the subterranean tasting rooms they had drunk wine of a vintage which General von der Linde had especially recommended. What was left of it the Killer had quickly swallowed, and he said that while it was not French wine, it had a flavor, it was a little fruity, and one had better get used to this flavor, because it was there for the taking, in infinite supply.

During some more wine tasting they got into a mellow mood. The German General said that he was happy about one thing and that was that he had been able to persuade the kitchen staff at Hohenlinden to remain.

He gave the signal of the gourmets, the index finger and thumb arranged into a ring and the eyebrows lifted, and

he said that the kitchen here was fantastic—"Wait until
you taste it." The kitchen was under the direction of Frau
Lampe, famous for her cooking. A woman worth her
weight in gold, specializing in solid, plain food, simply
cooked.

She was the high priestess of cooking, and the General
said: "As far as I am concerned—much more important
than the beaux arts, or sports, or politics, for the welfare of
a nation is die Kochkunst. Look at France, another country where it is esteemed." They clinked glasses again, and
for once Papa said: "D'accord."

"Now then, I must warn you, Your Excellency Herr General, she has a temper."

Papa smiled, indulgently; he understood.

"Any good cook worth her salt has," he said. It was late
now. Papa would pay a visit to the kitchen the next day.

After the inspection, Papa had ordered the Killer to take
the General to his house in town, and he said that von der
Linde had dismissed him with the same degree of cold
arrogance that he got year in year out from our father. He
said they were all the same and had regard only for their
kind. One should let them fight their wars with tin soldiers
or in the field and leave the rest of the world in peace. And
to have this frog of a man, this skin of the tanned bottom
of a pig, giving orders to a French soldier was the limit.
You know that big slice of a mouth he has, it's from giving
commands. He yelled from the back seat like a castrated
cock, this way, that way, left, right, straight on, in his boche-
flavored French, and at the end no thank you, no smile,
just imagining himself back in his almightiest position. He
stepped out, threw a stiff salute, and went into the house
where he lives. . . . And the eyes of all the Germans, seeing

this peau de vache, sitting in a French staff car . . . the
traffic policemen giving us swift passage and saluting—not
the French flag, not me, but the Schwein in the back seat.
Ça alors.

Hugo and Alain looked as disgusted as the Killer. And
that's supposed to be one of the good ones. He was in on
the plot to kill Hitler, and he showed us where he hid in
the vaults below. One could hold out there with wine and
food for years, and naturally there was also plumbing—
the Germans are thorough.

"Alors—then, I have my belly full, I have it up to here,
this occupation—"

Hugo and Alain and I agreed with him. He had brought
a bottle along and we drank and he said:

"Imagine clinking glasses, and the General saying to the
General how glad he is that Hitler is dead, what a piece of
fortune for Germany and the world—and he said that the
other German Generals that were in the plot had been
tied with piano wire and hung up on butcher's hooks, on
the wall, and left there to die slowly. Hitler came to look
at them while they hung there still alive. It seems to me the
worst ones, the rats, got away."

2. FRAU LAMPE

IT WAS EARLY, seven o'clock, and layers of fog drifted over the Moselle. On the way to the castle, the Killer reminded Papa that the first thing he had said he would do was visit the kitchen. This was because General von der Linde had told him how very agreeable the cooking was.

Papa was a military gourmet, he liked good food and would drive far to get to a restaurant where they made a dish to his liking. But always mindful of his figure, he ate very carefully, very little, and preferred plain things to rich ones. He especially liked vegetables, salads, and fresh fruit. He wanted to combine the visit to the kitchen with brief instructions to the cook. I was taken along because I had turned the pages of a German dictionary and knew a few phrases of the language, and this was a sort of visite de famille, rather than a military one. Mama, of course, in the Spanish tradition, had never been in any kitchen anywhere and would not come now.

Hohenlinden was a romantic castle such as one imagines along the Rhine and the Moselle, with battlements and towers that once had been of use in war. It had a façade toward the Moselle that made it look like an ivy-colored ruin when seen from below, but when one came up the winding road, it had another face. From that side, it was still castle, but very modern. In front of it was a parking place big enough to use as a parade ground. It had an immense garage, a park with a swimming pool, and inside everything except the furniture was modern.

There were immense halls, a Rittersaal—as the large salon was called—carved ceilings; the outstanding characteristic of the place was an abundance of lavatories everywhere. Almost every door we opened contained one with immense porcelain fittings, most of them for the use of men. Wide stairways, again carved, overlarge rooms with dressing rooms and elaborate baths.

Papa had sent the Killer down to inform Frau Lampe, the cook, that he was coming. Frau Lampe sent word that she was at the General's orders. We went down.

The kitchen was in the basement. Frau Lampe was in front of her oven and in back of her was her staff. It was as if they were a battery of heavy artillery drawn up for battle. Frau Lampe was immaculate, as was her kitchen, and a very unusual woman: a figure made of sacks of flour, and a pink, egg-shaped balloon of a head on top of which golden noodles seemed to be stacked. She looked like something a mad baker might have created, an immense, swollen loaf of flesh, moving on wheels, on rounded calves which spilled over her shoes. She moved with deliberate and majestic ease, rowing the air with her solid round arms—she was like the Grand Romulus getting under way. She turned and waved at her staff, and called out their names: Frau

Scheitholz, Frau Kueppersbusch, Frau Unterer. These were
the senior assistants, and then came Anneliese, Gertrude,
Hildegard, and half a dozen others, and from the pantry
appeared two stout scullery maids, and out of the "walk-in"
icebox a butcher, Herman Nickel, who came to sharp attention with a loud "phlump" of his rubber boots. Frau
Lampe put them at ease by saying:

"Tya—macht nur weiter Kinners."

She used "Tya" instead of the German Ja, and she said
"Kinners" instead of Kinder, which is dialect. Even with
her as a yardstick, the Kinners were a solid group, not out-
rightly unfriendly at this presentation, but not happy
either, and looking with quick glances at Papa when he
did not look at them.

The kitchen was spotless, and in the old tradition with
an immense oven in the center of the white-tiled room.
Frau Lampe said:

"Tya, here we cook with coal—not gas or electricity."

She had one complaint, the water in the neighborhood
contained a great deal of chalk. Water was very important,
and the water in that basin was for cooking only—she never
used tap water. The water of the region was hard, and even
this water, which came from the Black Forest springs of
Freudenstadt, had a content that formed "Kesselstein" and
therefore the Wasserschiff, as the container for this water
was called, was always kept meticulously clean inside and
out. Frau Lampe did not like anything newfangled, and
when Papa told her that I spoke some German, she gave me
a brief nod and went into giving a lecture on the oven:
Tya, she had it installed herself, she was here for twenty-
three years now, and as one could see everything had been

thought of—the oven was accessible from four sides, old-fashioned, heated with coal, and in her opinion, only Stein-kohle was acceptable as a fuel for a Küchenkohlenherd.

Papa looked at the largest copper casserole that stood on the oven, and Frau Lampe explained that this was the stock-pot, and that just as the oven was the altar of the kitchen, the stockpot was the heart; and half the battle in good cooking was won when the stock was good, and only the best materials went into that; and there were no recipes, no theories, no things that one could read in books—it came only by long and bitter experience—the art of making stock —and there could be no good stock, she said meaningfully, without the best materials—and then the good things would come. Tya—that is all about this pot of stock. She went back to her lecture on the oven.

There are few people even in Germany who understand the proper care of a Küchenkohlenherd. The Ofenkehrer has to come at least twice a year and clear the ducts. The surface of the oven is cleaned with a moist rag and sand every day, then washed, then rubbed in with a little oil, and polished—Tya Tya—but then what comes out of such an oven, Fräulein? Well, you will see what comes out of it!

"Tya und here—come here for a second, Herr General. Here is the bake oven and Frau Holle, the pastry cook, and her assistant Gretchen. Tya, the big Backofen, and the table for making applestrudel, and tarts and cakes and cookies, and above that the things like kettledrums in which to whip up creams, and the stuff for soufflés—Tya we have everything. . . ."

Papa was very pleased with the inspection and was ready to go. He bowed toward Frau Lampe and he told me to convey his pleasure to her and how very glad he was that she was at the castle.

The brigade of assistants around her all stopped what they were doing, the way a mechanical toy with many figures stops working. One held the rag he was cleaning with to the spot he was cleaning; another, who had bent over a pot stirring, remained bent but stopped stirring and looked up; a third, who was carrying something, carried but stood still; and only Herman Nickel clapped himself to attention again, also mechanically twisting his head to look at the General, and although he was now a civilian, he held a stiff salute. Papa answered his salute and the hand slapped itself down to the side of his trousers.

"Tya—" said Frau Lampe. She was honored that His Excellency the Herr General had come down into her kitchen, and she was sure that Hohenlinden would please him. She was able to feed up to two hundred people at a time here—and this hospitable house had had under its roof some very important people. The Führer himself had slept here—Marshal Goering, also Herr von Ribbentrop.

Papa suddenly became himself, his bonhomie left him, and he took his stance, pulled at his gloves, and said:

"I hope that you have changed the linen since."

"Tya, natürlich," said Frau Lampe.

For an instant the whites of the eyes of Frau Lampe had enlarged and there seemed another face on her body. The egg-shaped curves became disturbed and shifted, and the mouth was pressed into a straight line. Then she turned to the "Kinners" and in a sergeant's voice ordered them to get on with their work, and the mechanical toy started again, pounding, turning, stirring, and polishing.

3. GUTEN APPETIT

THE FIRST DAY, Frau Lampe sent up various Schlemmer-schnitten and belegte Brötchen. French champagne was served. There was a small reception for some of the French officers and their wives. They had been stationed in Wei-marein for some time, and the wives talked about their do-mestic problems. They were people who had lived in small circumstances in France and now had many servants, and they were all full of praise with what a treasure their Friedas or their Paulas or their Annelieses were, and how cheerful they were, and how they worked—they actually came and asked for more work when they had finished their tasks—and the cleanliness, and the kitchens—all bright—and the children all clean.

Mama listened to it all and at the end she said to Papa that it was all well and good for them, but as for us it was not right. Had he looked at the buffet that had been set up? The belegte Brötchen and Schlemmerschnitten with pickles on them—of each of these enough for a laborer's meal. Before deciding on the staff she suggested that he think twice. She said that to have them dispersed among other new French families, and for us to send for our chef might be the thing to do. Monsieur Benard knew what Papa liked; he had his tempers but it was better to have it that way.

One could never tell anything to Papa—he walked along not listening—he only knew how to give orders. He always said that he would think it over but he never did. He made his decisions instantly and then came the famous "I have said what I have said," and this time he had said that he would be happy having Frau Lampe stay on, so that was settled. For the house we needed a housekeeper. Mama was helpless without someone to direct things and look after the servants.

Mama said, with slightly distended waxen nostrils, "I think that this whole occupation is a great mistake—I feel it." Mama had antennas and believed in horoscopes and her intuitions.

Besides the military staff a dozen outdoor employees were busy as gardeners, carpenters, and in the services which the house needed. Those immediately around us—the upstairs and downstairs maids—were eleven. When we passed them on the stairs or in a corridor they acted as if they wanted to disappear; they pressed themselves against the wall hoping to fade into it. They never looked at us.

My mother in the Spanish tradition needed a major-domo and there was nobody to be hired that she liked. The Killer was the property of my father, and my mother kept him at a distance, for once she had called him in her very cultured Spanish accent and looked for him. He was above her on a wall, and he had jumped down the fifteen feet, which, with his parachute training, he did like stepping off a chair. That had frightened her. She was to be approached with dignity. The house in Beaufort had run itself but here she needed someone, especially since Papa would be any day the Commanding General.

There was no such thing as a proper major-domo in Germany; female housekeepers were the only alternative and Papa gave orders to advertise for one. In the meantime, Mother had to get along with her maid and Caroline, who had been taken along to help out in general.

Then came the first meal at the castle of Hohenlinden. The Killer announced:

"Madame is served."

We walked into the Rittersaal. There were two maids and a butler for the wine. Mama looked at everything with her nostrils waxen, her eyes indigo and hopeless. At this immense refectory table and in these chairs, once one was seated one sat. There was no way of pushing them closer, they were as if made of cast iron.

Mama nodded. The service began.

One would never think that one could reduce in Germany—but we all lost weight, on account of too much food.

Our first meal at Hohenlinden was the start of many sessions that raised your pulse, gave you expansions in the stomach, a feeling of strangulation, and when you looked at the cook you got vertigo in addition. The first meal was a salad of head of veal, then a soup with little eyes of fat floating on it, and with parsley chopped into it; submerged in each plate lay a gray submarine-shaped liver dumpling. Then came a roast stuffed goose, with red cabbage, and applesauce and salad served at the same time, and potatoes. Always Kartoffel. The dessert was a gruesome cold paste, dye-colored red and called Rote Grütze. The coffee was served at the same time as the dessert in large cups and with milk. We exchanged hopeless looks while all this was brought in. I thought of the pensionnat, and how I would like to throw my plate on the floor. We barely touched the food. At the end Frau Lampe came in, propelled herself to where Papa sat, and, leaning forward from her buttocks, ignoring us, and looking at Papa, she said:

"Hats nicht wohl bekommen, Herr General?" which means, "has it not become you well." Frau Lampe was used to having her food appreciated, and she liked to see the plates clear and empty with nothing but bones on them —also, what was los? She gave the explanation herself—the change of air and the excitement, that was it.

"You have to get used to my cooking, and when you are used to it, you will like it," she said. Everybody did and we were no exception. "Tya—better appetit the next time."

We had observed her entrance with great amusement, for we had expected an explosion. We had hoped to see Papa in action, reducing Frau Lampe to a trembling carcass and kicking her downstairs forever.

However, nothing happened; he looked at her with the kindest face he could manage, and wiping his mouth with his napkin—and adjusting his mustache—he said:

"Excellent, Frau Lampe."

Papa always made a point of remembering the name of the people under him.

He didn't even ask that black coffee, in small cups, be brought into the salon, or on the terrace.

Mama, who had eaten black bread and salad, and had not touched anything else, looked ill. We had eaten some goose. The wine was good, if a little sweet. We all got up, silently, and went out. To avoid any discussion, Papa quickly drove off with Auguste. He explained later to Mama that he could not fire the cook or the rest of the help the first week we were there—it would look very bad. He would adjust things and soon the menus would be in order. He commanded us to have patience. After all it was a foreign country, and they did their best.

The Killer said that Frau Lampe was mean to her staff. She had surrounded herself with a kitchen crew as awful as herself: all of them tough and unsympathetic. Down below in their kitchen they were like a cast of monsters waiting to go on in a fairy tale.

The problem was dealt with in various ways. Papa, who inclined to vegetables, asked for spinach, carrots, celery, and asparagus, but when they came to the table, they were not to his liking. Frau Lampe managed to make vegetables unpalatable by cutting them in a fashion to which we were not accustomed, or presenting them so they were floating in butter or covered with bread crumbs or awful to taste— or even to look at—and impossible to eat. Also they said they could not get this or that at the market or at the commissary, although we saw that it was to be had in stores and got it at other houses. It was no use complaining. Anyone talking to Frau Lampe now got a hysterical look and was menaced by the arms held out like a fat crab about to pinch you. She had changed completely.

Mama lived off some things her maid prepared. Finally Papa had the courage to tell General von der Linde that he did not have the palate to appreciate Frau Lampe's cooking—and neither did any of the rest of the family.

The General was very surprised and a little hurt. He brought a French cookbook that had been translated into

German: the Killer was to take it to Frau Lampe. She looked at it, held it in her hands, leafed through it for several minutes, got redder and redder, and finally threw it on the kitchen table and walked off and up to her room. She came back in time to cook a supper of what she took to be light cooking in the French manner. It too was inedible.

Papa answered this by having her informed that he was on a very strict diet and that Caroline knew exactly how his food was to be prepared.

It was all contained in a long memorandum. Papa stated that Caroline had been with us for years, and had helped out in the kitchen at Beaufort, and that she would prepare his meals, naturally under the supervision of Frau Lampe. Frau Lampe shook her head, but she assigned a corner of the huge oven to Caroline, and a few casseroles, and Caroline started cooking for Papa there. Frau Lampe and her crew stood around Caroline as she prepared the vegetables, and they made remarks in German and laughed bitterly and shrugged their shoulders.

We hardly ate anything of what came to the table. That is we took a little part of this or of that. We were hungry, and some of it, once you stopped hating it, wasn't too bad to eat. There is no worse punishment for a cook than having things sent back to the kitchen untouched—or plates half full of food not eaten. Frau Lampe became furious and shot her eyes into the dishes as they came back. Finally, by a process of elimination, she had reduced the menu to simple things like plain consommé or soups without "Einlagen," as the dumplings, marrow bones, Schinkenflecken, or other additions were called. Schnitzels, plain or à la Viennoise we liked (à la Holstein, with a fried egg, we sent

back and it never came again). A kind of German fricas-
sée de volaille, also a Gulash with sour cream and sauerkraut, were good, so was Rostbraten with onions, and plain
salads. With the exception of compotes we refused all des-
serts and "Torten." Torten were the specialty of the house,
and in the beginning they came in unbelievable sizes and
in colors, like nail enamel and plastic toys, or covered with
all kinds of glacé fruit and frosting.

If Papa had had the courage to talk to Frau Lampe in the
kitchen, it would have perhaps been possible to eat. But
now she felt unappreciated and neglected, and she had become hostile.

As it was the kitchen was an unpleasant place and hard
for poor Caroline to work in. When she wanted something
she was screamed at. They did not make any effort to be
nice or to understand, and they made it difficult for her.
When she asked for pepper they gave her nutmeg or cinnamon, and amused themselves with her helplessness. After
she got through cooking, although there were two scullery
maids, they left her pans and pots dirty where she had left
them. She was too nice to complain, and simply cleaned
them herself.

4. REINHILD AND HITLER

THE BUSINESS OF MOVING the army part of his command into Weimarein was a comparatively simple matter. It was organized like any military action and came off smoothly. With the exception of Frau Lampe and her crew, everyone was as happy as could be expected.

My parents lived on the first floor. I moved into two immense rooms and bath on the second floor and my brother chose a kind of student mansard under the roof and a study in the tower. There would have been rooms to house fifty more people in complete privacy.

On the day when our horses were brought and the last of the staff moved into the smaller houses on the property, Papa, waiting for the guard to mount, stood on the vast terrace overlooking the Moselle, and he saw a beautiful large German shepherd dog near the gate. Papa was very fond of big dogs and he called the dog. The dog came running, barking with joy, and moving like a rocking horse with extravagant jumps and twists and with his bushy tail waving. As he came to Papa he stopped very smartly and turned, so as to stand at his side, and he held up his head, so that it was easy to caress him. My father admired him immensely and talked to him, and patted his head and his back. The dog weaved around him and held Papa's hand in his teeth and looked at him with much intelligence and friendship. This went on for awhile, and then Papa thought that this was enough and told him to run along.

The guard had arrived, the soldiers had been moved into line in front of him. Again he told the dog, with some impatience now, to run along. The dog turned his head as if to understand Papa's French better, and Papa patted him once more, but then, as he stopped, the dog wheeled—and with his tongue hanging out from all the excitement, and looking as if he were laughing, he lifted his leg and wetted Papa's cavalry boots. This was very hard on the soldiers who now stood at attention and therefore could not laugh. To Papa it was a great surprise. He had his stick in hand as always, but he did not use it. He called the Killer who had stood by and had seen what had happened. The Killer offered to shoot the dog, but Papa said, "No—under no circumstances. Take him and lock him up for the time being."

The dog belonged to a German and the dog's name was Hitler. He was famous all through Weimarein. It seemed that the German had trained him to do this trick, and that he had had a good deal of amusement out of it—and had also almost lost his head during the Nazi time. The dog, of course, had no way of telling French officers from Germans, and the Germans were equally amused by one or the other. The story about Papa's boots was all over town. Something had to be done, for the Army of Occupation could not afford to make itself ridiculous in front of the conquered, and if something like this happened at a review, a parade, or some other show, then it would be disastrous.

At such times, Papa continuously hit the sides of his riding boots with his stick. After awhile he called the Killer and Auguste. On such nonmilitary matters, he talked to them as if they were human beings. They stood with him when he said that something had to be done with the dog, because it was a fine dog. The chauffeur was lip reading, and he nodded and said: "D'accord, mon Colonel" and the Killer said: "Yes, mon General, but what?"

Papa settled everything promptly. He said to the Killer: "You will take the dog, and you will train him. You know how to work with animals. I leave the method up to you. I don't want the animal's spirit broken. I don't want you to use a stick or a whip—and no chemicals or electricity—do it with kindness: animals respond to that like people."

"Ah oui, mon General," said the Killer, "but please tell me—comment il faut le faire?"

Papa got mad, and said: "What I have said, I have said —go now."

He turned on his heel and marched off.

Whoever appeared to visit the castle was stopped by the soldier at the guardhouse gate below. There the visitor had to state his business. Then the corporal of the guard telephoned up and stated the facts. And only then was the visitor allowed to enter the grounds—or else was turned away.

Shortly after the episode with Hitler there presented herself at the guardhouse below the person who was sent to fill the post as housekeeper. She identified herself and was admitted. It was rarely that anyone made the steep ascent to the castle on foot, but she arrived marching, ramrod straight, and was taken to headquarters. Mama was not to be disturbed until noon and therefore Papa would interview her first and pass on her qualifications. Her papers were thoroughly checked at headquarters and then she was escorted to the castle to meet Papa. She had a great many letters of recommendation.

Reinhild was thin, dry, and tall, with large hard hands. She was severely dressed, wearing a small cloche, a gray woolen suit, sensible black shoes, and black gloves. Her face was long, there was a straight line for a mouth. Perhaps a German officer's wife, I thought as she advanced to my father's desk—and with very large feet. He stood up. She raised a large hand in the Nazi salute and said: "Heil Hitler." We would have been beaten half to death, and soldiers locked up in dark prison cells, but Papa was forever unpredictable and in the case of women, that is all except me, very gallant. After a pause of shock he offered her a seat and said:

"Madame, if I understand you right, you wish to let me know that you were a Nazi."

She stood up again, and I thought she would salute once more and say "Heil Hitler" but she merely stated in her grating voice and in correct French:

"Not only have I been a Nazi, mon General, I still am one."

My father got up and said:

"My respects to you, Madame, you are an honest woman, and the first Nazi I have met in Germany. Please be seated."

He told her about the need of having discipline among the German help in the house, and that Mama would go over details with her. She listened fascinated, with her

gray eyes on my father intense and burning like those of
Monsignor Felice. He took her up to Mama, but at the
sight of her Mama got very cold and said that she was
sorry but that the position had been filled. Coming down,
my father said that he had changed his mind. Papa had
studied the references, and among them there was one that
said that the applicant had been a teacher and also a governess. He called me to the desk and said:

"Madame, you will be the governess of my daughter.
This is she."

Reinhild looked at me and I at her, and then my father
stated again the need for discipline and order, absolute
obedience inside and out of the house, supervision of
studies and exercise, his whole plan for bringing up
children. I felt that Reinhild and Papa loved each other
already. The thin line in her face that was her mouth soft-
ened as she looked at him. She would move in tomorrow
and bring her things. She chose a room next to me to sleep
in.

When she was gone, I said: "Please, Papa."

Papa said: "I have said what I have said—I never change
what I have once said—out with you! Go!"

I ran out. Reinhild was walking down the stairs and I
called out: "Hitler." She turned and stood frozen, and then
when Hitler came prancing out of the garden and jumped
up on me, I said to myself, "Well, the first shot was mine
and it hit the target." Hugo and Alain were practicing
knife throwing on a board in the garden, on which a human figure was outlined. The Killer was giving them lessons. I walked over to them and told them what had
happened, and they said not to worry, we would get rid of
Reinhild in short order.

She arrived with luggage that had a small crown on it and a "v" for "von" between her initials, and I suppose if I had bothered to find out what her name was, and title, and called her by that, things would have gone better but I chose "Reinhild," and since we can't pronounce "h," I said it "Reinild." She was worse than a daily beating. She gave me the cold-water treatment, she pulled my hair when doing it, and she never smiled or spoke kindly. She was a military martyr. She had a cot placed in her room instead of one of the large comfortable wood-carved beds. The other piece of furniture was an immense antique clothes closet, built in and too large to get out of the room; it would have had to be taken apart. She put everything she wore in her crested wardrobe trunk, as if ready to move out any day.

My mother asked who "that" was, having forgotten that she had met her before. I told her that it was Reinhild my new governess, and couldn't she do anything about it—I didn't need a governess. As usual my mother ignored me.

I ate with my brother in the Trinkstube. Reinhild ate alone in one of the smaller rooms on the ground floor. We waited for what would happen. There was one thing I must be grateful for—that I have snow-white teeth. I had to brush them after every meal with a hard brush and powder.

The Killer cured Hitler of his bad habit by patience and kindness. He asked Papa for an old pair of his riding boots, and he put them on, together with riding breeches and a jacket to go with the whole thing, and so dressed, like a general, he took long walks with Hitler in the forest and on the property, and whenever Hitler came running and wagged his tail and wheeled to get in position, the Killer held him by his head, and talked to him nicely, saying, "Nicht gut, non non—mustn't do that!" and Hitler seemed to understand. The first few times Hitler complained bitterly, barking up and looking sideways at the Killer, with eyes big with hurt, but he stopped his bad habit and went to visit trees and corners of buildings instead.

Hitler brought us good luck. In the days that he was training him, the Killer went all over the big terrain of Hohenlinden and the dog led him to a hidden place.

5. THE TOWER

AT THE VERY LAST PROMONTORY, atop a rock overlooking
the town of Weimarein, the Moselle, the bridge, the whole
of the Moselle Valley for miles down and up, stood a stone
tower. It rose some two hundred feet above the railroad
tunnel; below it were the shining tracks, signal lights, and
switches. From it one had a view of the mountains, and
also of every road that came into the town.

The Killer had come upon it by walking Hitler for
hours in his training exercises. There was also a more direct
route via one of the long tunnels, from the basement of the
castle. Following this tunnel one came to an iron door,
and opening this, suddenly stood in a tree-shaded glade
with rocks and a bench, and a shed with cooperage tools,
a kiln, and wood that had an acid taste from being soaked
in brine. From the toolshed one reached the tower in a
few steps. At the other side of the tower, there was a gate,
and a winding path descended through woods to the main
road. The tower was a romantic ruin outside, like the
castle, intentionally kept so and overgrown with ivy.

It was like a summer house, octagonal and with a tall spire. Inside it was like a German restaurant. Above the windows were murals of the Nibelungen tales, painted with a very sentimental brush. Against these on rows of shelves were drinking mugs, cups won for bowling, and bowls in which to mix wine and fruits. There was a large oak table, carved chairs such as one sees in Rathskellers, and over the table a strong lamp like those over gaming tables. The windows were all of stained glass showing scenes of German sagas, such as Lohengrin with his swan. There was a pantry with a refrigerator and a rotisserie, a stove, and iceboxes for wine and food.

A winding stone stairway covered by a trap door of metal-framed oak planks led down to a basement of the tower, and an iron gate of strong construction opened into the dank place of stone, which at one time must have been used as a prison, for heavy iron rings were on its walls. The Killer had the keys to the padlock on the gate. Here he kept tins of gasoline, extra tires, garden tools and his belongings, and black-market stores.

One could come here and get something to eat in spite of Reinhild. I went by way of the tunnel and the tower to go to my German lessons and Musikstunde, and any time I could invent an excuse to escape her, I stopped to eat there. There was always something—buttered crumpets, jam, tea, coffee, milk, or a glass of wine—and then on a path at the other side of the tower I ran through the woods down to the town. It was a short cut which allowed me to spend some ten minutes for stilling my hunger and thirst.

When the Killer wasn't busy with Papa and General von der Linde, he was busy with this, our secret hiding place. He drove with his jeep, and furnished it with anything we needed; the first thing he brought was a dart board and some very fine, balanced steel darts. Then he found that there were exquisite throwing knives to be found in Germany. The next discovery was canned foods in the American sector. Also he had been to a drugstore there, and he got things one could not buy in our part of Germany. He instituted a type of cooking which we were unfamiliar with, but which we took to immediately, and preferred to our French sauce cookery or the impossible cuisine of Frau Lampe. This came from the Americans and consisted of very simple things like ham and eggs, bacon and eggs, hamburgers or hamburgers with spaghetti, and Spam, and sauces like catsup. Then there was ice cream, which he brought in Thermos containers, and American cigarettes, American lipstick, American stockings—we had everything American except the American flag flying from the top of the tower. We had a very happy time together here—Alain and Hugo, Veronique, the Killer, Hitler, and I.

We met there for the midday meal, and also late at night, everyone escaping from the castle. Outside my bedroom window, there was a ledge, and by moving along this sideways for some ten feet, I could get to the hall window and down the backstairs to the basement and out to the tower, and could come back that same way without Reinhild knowing where I was.

There were other things we needed besides the food which the Killer got from the American sector. We ate all our meals at the tower and that took a lot of supplies. For those he went to the kitchen, and whenever he did so he had difficulties with Frau Lampe. Without asking for her permission or that of Herman, the guardian of the refrigeration, he simply walked in and helped himself to anything in the kitchen and the icebox, and then handed it to Caroline if it was not too heavy, and told her to carry it to the tower. Then Frau Lampe put her arms across her chest and locked them there and she told him in German that she was in complete charge of the kitchen, and he said, "Tya—tya—I know that," and he tweaked her cheek and was off. The first time he did that was all right, but the second time Frau Lampe had in her hand a big heavy iron pole with which the fires are stirred, and she stood as if she were going to hit the Killer when quickly he tweaked her again. Then she wanted to see Papa, but he was out, and a captain told her that as long as the Killer filled out a slip he was allowed to take whatever he wanted. After that the Killer just signed the slips and told Frau Lampe to fill them out herself.

Then the Killer started bringing things instead of taking them. One day the Killer came in carrying a huge boar he had caught on his infernal machine. The forest was close by. The Germans had had to give up all their hunting things—guns, traps, knives. The forest was filled with wild boar, deer, pheasant, and rabbits. He came in with the boar slung over his shoulder, and without asking permission walked past her, opened the walk-in refrigerator, and hung the boar on a meat hook. Then, again without asking permission, but with a hard smile, he took the knives he wanted and started sharpening them, all the time looking at Frau Lampe as if he were getting ready to butcher her; one wondered when and how the explosion would come and what weapons they would use. At the end he did a few tricks to confuse them all, throwing a heavy kitchen knife in a series of loops, and making a butcher cleaver spin and catching it by its handle. The kitchen help stood looking bewildered, the one other expression they had besides being unpleasant.

Frau Lampe shook her fist at the Killer and told him to stay out of her kitchen. She had had a sign made and she pointed to it now. Herman would bring him anything and also hand him anything he wanted across a kitchen table which she had placed at the door. The Killer whistled, smiled at her, and went into the refrigerator.

The next day he was found half frozen in the refrigerator. Frau Lampe said that the door must have closed accidentally, and that she was so glad that he was found in time—and so was her crew—although they looked very depressed. Alain wanted to report it, but the Killer said that he preferred to settle the matter in his own way. He said, talking of his experience in the icebox:

"I was locked up with a half-dozen suckling pigs, hanging from the hooks; they looked so naked next to my wild boar—which was luckily immense. I had my knife with me and I skinned him and covered myself with his pelt. And Caroline came down early to get milk and cream for the Corn Flakes, and she let me out."

Corn Flakes were something new and American and for Hugo. He ate them, slicing bananas over them, and the first time I heard that I thought it was autumn and that someone was walking through dead leaves.

"Will you kill Frau Lampe?" Alain asked the Killer.

"Oh no," said the Killer. "I won't do anything to her, it's all been done. Sitting there last night and looking up at the pigs hanging there, I thought how it was all as it should be. They had been pigs and now they would be eaten, and gone, but the butchers were still here, and all their lives they would have to butcher pigs and work with their bloody aprons. Have you ever seen them, around les Halles in Paris, in the winter with their blue hands and their rubber boots, and running for a drink—and having to live the way a butcher lives—all his life a butcher with all the troubles of old age coming on him, and sickness and misery? No, the part of the pig is preferable, and I think that killing anyone or committing murder is idiotic. It's much more punishment to let them live. Look at Frau Lampe, at General von der Linde—look at everyone."

"Tiens—listen—the Killer has become a philosopher," said Hugo. "Do you feel all right—did you drink a lot?"

"No, no—I didn't drink," said the Killer. "I feel fine. I am very happy to be alive."

The Killer started to cook, and it all at once began to smell of ham and eggs and fried potatoes. We put on a record and were very glad to be in our tower.

6. PLAY WITH SOLDIERS

"The rats were in the cheese last night, and what a time they had, vachement sympat—vachement trance— terrible." The Killer was pale. "Last night's Kriegspiel went on until four in the morning—they smoked, they drank. Your father fought the battle of Waterloo, Herr General von der Linde did Hindenburg in the Masurian Lakes, and then the German fought the Third World War. I had to clean up after and put the pins back. I'd rather shovel manure than go through another one of these campaigns.

It is unreal, the way this works. To see two grown men bent over a map, figuring out how many more of the other side one could kill with the greatest economy—to play at this for hours, one must have a very peculiar make-up—"

"It's simple when one likes being a general," said Hugo.

"However," added the Killer, "it is vachement sensas. It's still a mess down there now, and please come and help me put it in order. I can't read the German labels."

We waited until Alain came, and then we all went down

to the third subterranean vault, where the hall with the soldiers was located. A large fireplace was at the end of it. The Killer pushed one button among many and the walls lit up. They were covered with murals of famous battles which the Germans had won. Another button lit up the table, and there was the German-Russian border.

Soldiers were all over the fields: small shiny troops meticulously painted, with individual faces; infantry, artillery, cavalry soldiers, officers, and generals; a wonderful Napoleon group, with his famous field kitchen and the wagon he lived in.

"At the end yesterday, in one battle, the soldiers were all Poles, Czechs, Hungarians, and Germans," said the Killer, "and I must say, I have changed my mind about von der Linde—he's vachement sympat, once you know him. And he knows his business. That brain rolls, there are no brakes on it. Your father listened, and von der Linde did the talking and showed the plans."

"Tell us more," asked Alain. "What did they talk about?"

"Oh—they talked mostly about the annoyances of military life, the troubles with politicians, and the systems of promotion, and how lucky one was in having a private fortune large enough so that one was independent and could live well, for on general's pay it was not gay. But they never tire of playing soldiers. I went to get some cold meat for them and when I came back they had started on a new Kriegspiel. The maps here were much bigger than in Beaufort and specially mounted on cork so one can put pins into them easily. They placed the pincushion between them, and stuck in the pins to show how the regiments stood at the beginning of the battle. They moved their pins according to the way the battle went exactly like in Beaufort. They did Waterloo again—and General von der Linde informed your father that the real reason Napoleon lost that battle was not the rain but the fact that the French Emperor had had a very bad attack of hemorrhoids on the eve of the battle. Your father did not reply and seemed to resent the information. Then they got up and went into two rooms to which General von der Linde had the keys. In these were shelves of dioramas. The brother of General von der Linde had also been a secret collector who, like your father, showed his works to very few people.

"Anyway, it was interesting, and I know a few things about it now. It's a whole world, this, and they take it very seriously. They pick up figures and lovingly turn them and study the correctness of the uniforms, arms, and equipment."

"At last it was four o'clock and they had had enough. I drove the Herr General home then—and he thanked me and excused himself for keeping me up so late. Just the same, I would like to open his head," said the Killer, "to look inside to see where he really stands—one never knows these days. That's the terrible thing. In the old days a man was an enemy or a friend; now you don't know what he is any more, or what he will be tomorrow."

It took us hours to put the porcelain soldiers away, and while we were still at it Alain said to the Killer: "Listen to me carefully. When the Generals meet again, listen to every word that is said and report it to us."

Hugo said: "You are not spying on Papa?"

"Of course not. But I am very interested in General von der Linde and what he has to say."

So, whenever they met, the Killer came with his reports and I had to take down what the two Generals said. The Killer did it haltingly, saying many times "and then he said, and then the other one said," and the gist of these conversations was the following.

7. DIALOGUE

Dialogue A: The Hunter Wasp

GENERAL VON DER LINDE SAID:

I look for an explanation, for a reason, and I cannot find it. Sometimes, I think that perhaps we Germans are put in this world like a catalyst, to create disturbance, to stir things up. This same pattern, for example, exists in the animal world among insects.

Take the life cycle of the hunter wasp and the tarantula. The hunter wasp seeks the tarantula in its earthen hole, provokes it to come out, and stings it. This paralyzes the tarantula, whereupon the wasp deposits her eggs in its body.

The newborn wasps then feed off the tarantula, devouring it as they grow, and this living larder dies, having been made a shell, and the new hunter wasps fly off to repeat their performance. If whoever created this world took the time to design this minuscule vicious detail, why not play with humans the same way.

How is it possible that a race of men—likable in their normal state, kind to animals, morally clean in their personal lives, respectful, civilized, even cultured, and the most law-abiding citizen on earth—find themselves, at regular periods, turned into creatures as vicious as the hunter wasps. And mark you none but a handful, perhaps only the criminals in this society, are happy. For whatever his songs, and slogans, and loud-mouthed shouts, the German is not half as good a soldier, as, say, the American. He is a good soldier by obedience alone, and an unhappy one. There were, year in, year out, more suicides among German soldiers than in any other army. It is not, as is generally believed, part of their nature to shoulder guns and shoot. The peaceful Swiss are much more gun-loving. The Germans are at bottom too sentimental for that. They are flower lovers, music lovers, putterers in small gardens, family people of the most devoted pattern. Explain it to me. The psychologists flee into the domain of inferiority complexes, but that is too easy. All the explanations I have heard are too easy. Blame it on God, blame it on nature, on who else can you blame it?

He was not drunk, nor was your father, although by now I had opened four bottles. Oh yes, I forgot to tell you, there is a secret cellar to which the Herr General took your father, and there is the best Bordeaux, Burgundy, French champagne, everything—bottles and bottles of these—and they drank of these. That little General can drink an awful lot, and he smokes incessantly.

He then spoke on the problem of what would happen if the whole world were at peace for a thousand years, and both he and your father said that it was unthinkable, and that naturally the consequences would be fearful, for it would be the end of generals and the military. And so they agreed in the end that the Germans had to be the way they were and that it was their fate to make excellent enemies.

Dialogue B: On Being on the Right Side

This time the Herr General started to explain about the plans of the Nazis.

The Nazis everywhere, and that includes members of the Waffen S.S., are again in important positions in Germany, even in the government. The organization of the S.S. is as sharp, as thorough, as German organizations can be; it functions everywhere. Take the following case, for example.

There was a man who had been listed as missing for years, and who never came to trial in the war crimes courts. Actually he had only changed his name and he practiced as a family doctor, accredited as such in Munich. One day it was discovered that this doctor, under his real name, had been one of the commanders of the S.S. in the Dachau concentration camp, and that some thousand lives were on his conscience. The police were sent to arrest him.

The underground of the S.S. works so perfectly that not only was he forewarned, but, dressed as an Alpinist, with a rucksack, a set of new papers, and a passport valid for travel abroad, he was actually at the Starnberg depot as the police came to his house; he crossed into Austria, via Mittenwald, from there went to Vienna, and by plane to Egypt, where now he is functioning as a doctor, and waiting.

The Nazis say: In 1914 we had the Kaiser, and we lost

the war on account of the Americans. In the last war we had the Führer, and we lost again on account of the Americans. But in the next war we will win, and why will we win? Because this time we will be on the right side.

And what is the right side?

The right side is America.

Then the Herr General cleared away the pins of the Hindenburg campaign, and he changed the map so that we had before us all the countries from the North Sea to the Black Sea, and he said:

This is how the story goes now: The Russians are bluffing—theirs is the greatest bluff in the world and we alone can call it. They are scared to death of what will happen. They have already put up their own gallows. I speak now as the S.S., the Herr General said. The Russians have done the work for us—we all have but to wait a little longer and Der Tag will come as sure as tomorrow. The Russian bear will be hounded on all sides. The Russians are already the losers of the Third World War. We need no help from our allies, except that America holds the atomic umbrella over us, while we do the groundwork.

And given some time, we won't have to trouble the Americans for that even. We are very good at such things, and you know that the modern arsenal contains some surprises—especially in the department of chemistry—that are quick, efficient, and humane. I might say in this connection, dear colleague, that the Russian soldier is stoic and fatalistic about dying, and with good reason. As a soldier he is among the worst. Napoleon, if you remember, was defeated by snow and winter—not by military action. And so was Hitler.

Your father said: What about Stalingrad?

The Herr General did not answer but pointed to the map. We have here, he said, an immense fifth column that runs all along the frontier of Poland, Czechoslovakia, Hungary, and all the rest. They have frozen, starved, and beaten the laughter out of all these people. Only in their dreams do they see the good things of life. The Czarist-Communist imperialism has done a thorough job. And we hope they continue more thoroughly, so that the lessons of these years will never be forgotten. This is our greatest military asset.

When we come to their aid, we won't need any help. The Wehrmacht can do it alone—with the satellite nations properly supplied with weapons.

Oh, there may be small resistance here and there, but we will deal with that with proven methods; all that is marked and catalogued for X-Day.

This time we will come in the American tradition, as liberators; we will free them. Also we shall have the blessing of the industrialists, for they will think of the immense markets that are going to open to them.

The Herr General continued: I have told you all that is most important; I would keep you all night, explaining the rest of the logistics of this plan to you, for example, the position of Russia, which will have to worry about what China will do. The Russians are very concerned—that I know definitely—not about Berlin, which is merely a pawn, but about us, Germany.

Then your father asked what he himself thought of the plan, and there was another bottle and the Herr General said: Frankly, as a soldier, I think the logistics are sound. If they will proceed as the Americans do, and if they have the intention of liberating these people, I say it is a very good and right plan and a moral one—and moral is important to morale.

But in any plan there are unexpected things that may happen and change everything. There are two possibilities to consider which may wreck this plan, and they are, first—and that is remote—that the Russians will be intelligent enough to give the satellites their freedom, and withdraw, which would put these nations automatically against Germany. I don't think we have to worry about that.

The second—and that is very grave—is that one of the satellite nations will start a revolution and try to liberate itself. In that case the whole plan would collapse—or at least it would take years to get things in shape again.

Then your father asked what the Herr General thought the Russians would do if the plan were carried out in all its details and was successful. The Herr General said that on that point he would put his hand into the fire; nothing would happen. They are Asiatics, they would withdraw, they would weigh their chances, and they would find that it was a risk—and a real risk they never take. Take Tito and Yugoslavia. There is the perfect illustration—the territory frightened them, mountains are hard to fight in.

You know, the Führer asked his advisers once what it would take to conquer the Swiss. The answer was seventy divisions. For once the madman listened.

Then your father asked, would he, General von der Linde, go along with the plan?

He said: I would go along with the unification of Germany and the liberation of the slave nations. But I'm afraid it will not be like that with the S.S. They will turn into wasps again, it will be Deutschland über alles. They will march on to Moscow—they will do it with torture, with concentration camps, with their same methods—and we shall have it all over again.

Your father then said: What is the solution?

The Herr General said: I have thought of committing suicide so often, it's boring. You will find that in any German planning, there is no alternative but to do or die, and how to die they know very well. The plan marches forward, there is nothing to stop it. The Americans with their great benevolence help it along; the voice of America helps it. The Russians themselves help it most of all with their brutality—and the poor people in between, who are driven deeper and deeper into misery, what do they have to lose but their chains. Who said that? Marx, Engels, or someone like that—Lenin, I think—and not so long ago— and not about communism.

The terrible disaster that may grow out of it is not in their calculations. They die, then, like my poor brother, who owned this castle, who was a fanatical Nazi and a great friend of Hitler's, and who, when it was all over and there was no more hope, invited all his friends and with his family sat around the table up in the Rittersaal, and after a toast to Deutschland pressed a button and blew himself and all to the beyond.

Hitler, it may interest you, came here often and played with these soldiers.

Hitler the dog, when he heard his name, got up from his place near the fireplace, stretched himself, and walked over to the Herr General, who put his hand on his head.

The dog lowered his head as he scratched it, and the General lowered his head, and I think that he cried.

8. THE SILVERY PIKE

WE HAD LEARNED just enough German to say Moselblümchen properly, and then the woman who owned the
inn smiled, adjusted our pronunciation a little, and
brought the small carafe with the green golden liquid to
us in the garden of the inn under the blossoming linden
trees. This inn was a silent place of vineyards and fisher-
folk, serene and untouched by war. The Moselle turned
there in a wide arc, its waters mirroring the pale green
vines that covered the hills, the castle of golden stone in
which we lived up above, and the pale blue of the sky.
Swallows skimmed over it, and this moving silent mirror
was disturbed only when boys threw stones in it, or tried
to make them dance across the water. A blind man, led
by a dog, came toward evening. I could not imagine anything more beautiful in spring than the Moselle valley.

We walked along the riverbank often. I always took
Veronique home; we pushed our bicycles along the tow
path. The house which Colonel de Voltera had requisitioned was a very solid and imposing villa along the right

169

bank of the river, with a park, a swimming pool, and garages, and by the Moselle, a small boathouse with a rowboat. These long and narrow boats were kept along both sides of the river, chained to stone quays. There were also boat-shaped fishboxes, with holes in them and a padlock attached to the cover, in which pike, the most desirable fish found in these waters, were kept.

These small, unpainted boatlike and coffinlike shapes of wood, with long guirlandes of dark green moss trailing from their sides, rode silently submerged in the soft currents, and I felt sorry for the fish imprisoned in them and robbed of motion.

With his unequaled arrogance, Alain brushed away my concern. He said that the pike were the tigers of the river and that they killed fish and that everyone eats someone else in life. Nature was logical and simple and one should not complicate it with soggy sentimentality, and should be eating rather than be eaten.

He said then, looking at me with his hard green eyes that were like those of the pike, and never soft or begging, that he had no fear for me: "You're smooth and quick, and a smiling shark with your white teeth and blue-black hair. You'll never be eaten."

Evenings Veronique and I drank our Moselblümchen in the garden of a tavern called the Silvery Pike. We had been told by Reinhild never to go into the tavern itself.

The tavern had an entrance hall, a long corridor that led to washrooms, all tiled, cold, and clean. To the left was a dining room, which served the regular customers. On the right was the kitchen and pantry, and there was one door, through which, down a winding stair, one came to a cellar, which was vaulted, with a bar at one end, and

one of those out-of-tune pianos that are called piano
mécanique in France. The walls were of brick. Over the
bar were travel posters from all over the world, pasted
half over each other. There were paper lanterns and pictures painted by the members—for this was a club of
young people who read there, played jazz records, wrote
poetry, sang—all of them pronouncedly different from any
German one saw in the street. The street Germans were
poorly dressed and shabby. These were dressed with a
defiant neglect. They were like the young people whom
one sees around universities in France, and at the Beaux
Arts, the youths who have not enough money to eat or
dress properly. They were, both boys and girls, dressed
alike: trousers, sweaters, odd jackets, mufflers, and all had
a way of wearing their hair as unruly and long as possible.
They drank beer or the native wine. We never saw anyone
eat anything there, and they didn't look as if they ate much
anywhere else. They had, however, energy enough to dance
continuously to either the mechanical piano or the record
player, which played American jazz exclusively, or to an
accordion or mouth organ.

The Killer had heard of the place, and told us about it.
Once we discovered it they could not refuse us admission.
At the start, when we came in for the first time, all dancing
stopped. They seemed not to see us, but sat together in
small groups, at small tables, never turning to look at us
and remaining so until we left.

The woman who owned the place, or ran this club, was
a very little, very wiry person. She sent the waiter to the
table, a very Wagnerian boy, a blond Siegfried. He asked
us what we wanted. We said Moselblümchen. He brought
a small bottle, and we took out cigarettes and smoked

them. We paid and left. The next night we went there Veronique put on black velvet trousers and a sweater, and I, who was not allowed to have any pants, wore a long black skirt, also a black sweater and one of my brother's shirts, with the collar outside the sweater and the cuffs turned up outside the long black sleeves. We came in and the proprietress sat down and started to talk to us. She had a lovely face and she told us she knew France, Spain, and Italy, and that she had been an actress. She cautioned us, "Please! Be careful," for, she said, she did not want to have any trouble with the French authorities, and if our parents heard about our coming here there would be difficulties. The Germans did not look with favor on her. The club was under surveillance, but one had got used to that because, in Germany, everybody had for years been under surveillance, especially anyone who was different from the rest of the population. They certainly were different. The young people eyed us with cold inimical looks. The third evening we came they began to thaw; two boys asked us to dance, the place came to life. Some of them were rehearsing plays. Poets read their works, and the lady who had been an actress played the guitar and sang French songs. Then we all sang together. I asked my brother to get the latest records from the American sector. It was surprising that the young Germans were all devotees of American jazz, knew the words and the music of Duke Ellington, Count Basie, Dizzy Gillespie, Louis Armstrong, Sidney Bechet. They would get delirious over every new record. We had to sneak back home early. They said that around three in the morning they played classical music, and we tried to find a way to stay out that long. I managed to arrange for some late "German lessons," which in a sense

they indeed were, for we spoke German at the club. I
told Hugo about the place and asked him to come along.
He said he would not give me away, but that for him
there was no such thing as Germans with whom one sat
down and sang, or danced. Alain was furious when
Veronique asked him to take her, and she had to beg him
not to tell her father. We both made food packages, and
the German boys and girls ate with as much decorum as
their hunger allowed them; that is, they sat waiting until
Siegfried had divided the food, put it on plates, and
brought bread and knives and forks. Then they devoured
it.

As we got to know them better, we observed that in
this close society which packed the place at its small tables,
almost sitting on top of each other, there was a great deal
of conflict. While they were all held together by their
love of music and the fact that they were young and had
decided to be of the group, there were the quiet ones in
one corner, who had a little more money than had the
others. They sat drinking and staring into their glasses.
Some of them were with girls, sitting and holding on to
each other, both on one chair, as if to keep each other
from falling off. Then, although the room was under a
cloud of smoke, there were the naturists and health
seekers; boys who were obviously athletes, with very good
faces, undisturbed, and also sexless—and girls who looked
like skiers and athletes and also sexless. Those unable to
afford skiing trips went on hikes or rowed on the Moselle
in a shell owned by their club. They played darts, and
here we made our first mark on the group, for with our
training in throwing knives we beat them all. This group
drank herb teas and something they said was the best

medicine for cleaning out their already very clean bodies, which was tea brewed from the stems of cherries. They all had things they brought along and the cellar was a kind of refuge rather than a tavern.

Close to the bar sat those of political inclinations. There was the corner of the lofty intellectuals who discussed Pascal and psychoanalysis with us—and also their personal philosophy, the way they saw life, and the many problems of religion, of death, of love. Some were sad and filled with a great deal of self-accusation because of being German. Others said that while they were people who had been twice destroyed, they would, in spite of it, rise to be the strongest in the world.

In another corner were the flirts. There not a word was spoken—great silences—long deep looks—and if one got in there one got a pressing like a suit at the tailor's, and a massage by merely walking past. When one of them asked us to dance, it was like finding oneself in bed with them and we had to say, "Monsieur, please don't forget you are in a restaurant." They danced like hunchbacks, with elaborate twists and movements as if they were suffering from stomach cramps—or else wildly, with faces of tortured ecstasy. These invited us out to benches along the Moselle, or to lean us against a wall, or even to a cemetery which lay between the inn and our homes. They offered to take us home, and we allowed them to push the bicycles to a point a certain distance from home. Since there was the silhouette of the castle, and I was the daughter of the General, and Veronique was equally important or more so, because her father had the military police and the jail directly under him, it always ended with a comradely handshake and a proper kiss and Gute Nacht. The Nacht was not always so good, for once I met my father on the way up to the castle, and my explanation did not satisfy him and *paff paff*, I had a pair of slaps, and the visits to the tavern were over for awhile.

Reinhild came to see if I was in my room and in my bed, but after awhile the watchfulness was relaxed. When we came back, the club greeted us with shouts of joy, crying, Ah, our mascots are back. We brought cigarettes and sausages. There was a wonderful noise: the group that rehearsed screaming to be heard, the mechanical piano, "pickup," as the record machine was called, the various philosophical arguments, and the flirters and dancers; we had a place in which we were happy and nothing ever had been like it. There was mute adoration in Siegfried's eyes. And the actress sang a ballad to the tune of the "Marseillaise" that could have landed all of them in jail.

Hugo said to me one day not to go there that evening, for Alain had told him that the military police would check on the place. We raced down with our bicycles to warn them. When the French police came, they found some staid Germans upstairs, eating their sauerbraten and drinking Moselblümchen, and downstairs it was dark, quiet, and deserted.

9. PAPA'S PROMOTION

THE CASTLE WAS in furious excitement. Dressmakers from Paris had sent clothes for Mama. The tailor of the Ecole Militaire and Monsieur Guyomard the bootmaker, who made the finest officers' boots in France, were busy measuring and trying on. There were shirtmakers as well, and makers of kepis, insignia, flags, and painters of emblems. Papa was busy with all this and looked into mirrors wherever he went. The Killer kept addressing him as "mon General," although the promotion was a week off. A large party would be given after the official ceremonies of the Paradeplatz of Weimarein am Rhein. Tribunes were built, and the balcony in the center of the ancient Rathaus was reserved for the family and friends. From there we would see the three-hour festival of French military grandeur, with marching, massed bands, and then the decorating done by a General Sevignon, a very important General in line for his own promotion to Marshal of France. Everybody polished and brushed. The Killer and the chauffeur also got new uniforms, and looked at themselves in mirrors, and everybody rushed around giving orders and countermanding orders, and regimental music and trumpets blared; everywhere there was glory. The drill-ground sergeants bellowed and crowed, and the town itself started to join the fiesta, for who loves a parade and military goings on more than the Germans.

Two days before the great day, the other General came and the ceremonial was gone over and rehearsals held. There was also the small box in which the important medaille of the Grand Cross of this or that Order reposed, and this was like the rings at a wedding—which at the last minute everyone was afraid would not be in the groom's waistcoat pocket. To avoid this, it was decided to leave the medal at the castle for the time being, in Papa's room—since he would be the least likely to forget it—and in that they were very right. He showed it to Mama, who admired it. It had several diamonds stuck in it and they discussed its probable value. The Killer, who helped Papa dress for the rehearsal, told us all about it. On the nervous day before the promotion, my brother came to my room and asked me if I could sew. I said I could a little, like sewing on a button. That was all that was needed, he said. It was to be done on Papa's uniform. This new uniform was all laid out in his dressing room for tomorrow, but it needed a small addition.

The medal was there, too, and it had been decided that it would remain there until the last minute, in the box, and that then the adjutant of the new General would hand it to the adjutant of the General who came to decorate Papa—and the latter would take it from its box and then pin it on Papa while the band played the "Sambre et Meuse" and the guns roared. It was all very confusing.

My brother reached in his pocket and showed me the medal. He had already closed and wrapped the box. And now with needle and thread we would attach the medal where it belonged, to the seat of Papa's trousers, and for once we would enjoy a military ceremony.

This very simple thing done, we placed the uniform trousers exactly where they had been and where everything was laid out, from the new stick to the gloves, and left, hoping for the best.

Tara tara, boom boom tara—the making of a new general is one of those things that upsets everyone connected with it, and brings a very unusual mood to a place. It's like a canonization—and of cannon there had been plenty since the dawn.

Like all ceremony it makes me want to cry. It always reminds me of a picture I once saw, an old engraving of the degradation of Dreyfuss; it's as sad as that. The military units are always arranged in the same fashion. They stood so in the caserne at the Ecole Militaire on that disgraceful day, and now here they were again like toy soldiers taken out of their box and rearranged for a new ceremony.

Only Hitler cruises around freely and smells soldiers here and there, and everybody looks at him either hopefully or frightened, but he is behaving himself; perhaps he is waiting for the General with the medal. He is very clever; at least that is what Hugo and Alain and I hope. The buildings are beflagged; we are on our balcony in the center of the Rathaus. Flags on rooftops, flags in soldiers' hands, motorcycle orderlies racing this way and that, Hitler sprinting with them. The square fills up, all the important places are taken, and everyone is rigidly

expectant and looking at the people who are moving
around—and looking at the oncoming cars—and here
comes the new General, my father, very beautiful in his
glorious new uniform, his chest covered with ribbons—
he is elegant. He faces us, but gives no sign of recognition.
Hitler runs up to him, and my father finds time to pat
him on the head. People stand in back of him, but nobody
laughs.

"Patience," says Hugo to Alain, who knows the secret
of the medaille. . . . The French police troops are shoving
the Germans back against the wall and among these, like
a lost child, stands General von der Linde in his civilian
clothes. That wave of disgust I have for these things rises
in me. I look at the poor Germans—who have come to
do homage and who want to play with soldiers once more,
even though they're not their own—pushed back, pressed
against houses. But they don't seem to mind and they
all are elated, and they stand there patiently, with shining
eyes, the little ones held up by their parents. They expand
and then they are pushed back again; they are like waves
on the beach.

I say to Alain, "Ignoble," and he says, "Yes, you are
right—they should not have allowed them in." On that
point we will never agree; he doesn't understand me, he
has no idea of what I mean. Alors, now it begins.

Such ceremonies always consist of perpetual beginnings
in spite of the strict schedule. Now it really seems to
begin; my father moves forward onto the reviewing
tribune— Tara ta boom boom— There are too many
people around him; we cannot see the back of his uniform.
Now comes the General who will decorate him— He has
only one arm, which I always find statue-like and excit-

ingly heroic—like a face marked by scars, or a missing
hand—even German faces cut and sliced by sabers from
dueling—a black patch over an eye. All that is slashed
and has the stamp of something endured is attractive to me
—when it is worn with pride. So now they play the
"Sambre et Meuse"—and my backside aches in memory of
beatings and I feel like crying on account of Papa, who is
standing there like a little boy getting his reward. There
is the adjutant with the little box—and he opens it and
in alarm closes it again, for of course there is nothing in
it. I look at Hugo. Why do we play jokes like that? It's fun
to think them up, but not to do them. Poor one-armed
General de Sevignon looks into the empty box, too, but he
laughs, that is to say, he laughs in a military way. It's like
a dog thinking of giving a bite—he is known for his
discipline. The adjutant opens the box again and looks
once more, like a magician whose trick has gone wrong;
both the General and the adjutant look, and my father
also. It is a terrible moment. Poor men, the military
are always lost when they have no manual of instructions
about what to do. The music plays, and the people below
cannot see what is going on as they are blocked by the
shoulders of the blue devils and the other regiments.
Alas, there is no ruling that says how to proceed in case
the box in which the medal is, is empty. Falling back on
his own resources, General de Sevignon touches Papa's
shoulder with his sword, embraces my father, and makes
his brief speech, to which my father answers to cries of
"Vive la France—Vive la Gloire." Now starts "Allons
enfants de la patrie . . ." "Vieux peau de vache," says
Hugo. "Go now, General, show us your behind," says Alain.
The General bows to Madame la Generale de Sevignon,

and now it is clear that my brother made a terrible miscalculation—he did not allow for the very low drape of the tunic of a general's uniform, which completely covers the seat of the trousers. Even when he bends over, the medal remains hidden.

Now the marching begins, the square trembles, the Germans have tears in their eyes—and Hitler, with his bushy tail wagging, is at the right flank of the first line passing in review. He follows, proudly, and then he veers off, runs to the reviewing stand, well trained, ignoring all the boots there. The ceremony comes off well and passes without incident to its ending.

The rest of the festivities are moved to the castle. The caterers, who have come from Cologne to reinforce the help, are busy with preparations.

For us there was now the problem of how to get the medal off Papa's trousers and avoid the penalty for an amusement which had failed. The Killer said he would try to help Papa take the trousers off and so retrieve the medal, but he came too late. On account of the pressure and the many details, Mama had stayed with Papa in his dressing room to talk with him—in the intimacy of their rooms, she called him "mon petit loup." My father had taken off the tunic, and was about to go behind a German needlepoint screen of Wartburg Castle to remove his trousers, when Mama, who is farsighted, said:

"Wait an instant, my little wolf, there is something on the back of your trousers."

In such cases Papa always sent for me first. He was still in his dressing room when I arrived. He had taken off his trousers and laid them on the chaise longue, with the medal still attached to them.

He was in long, thin underwear, and all that was left of the General about him were his highly polished boots with spurs on them, which he had in his hand. He placed them on the floor and sat down to put his feet into his blue velvet slippers, on which the family crest was embroidered in gold. He looked at me, and with his mustache rising and in the nasal voice of the drill grounds, he snapped:

"Qui, qui a fait ça, hein?" jerking his head toward the trousers. Making the face I had at the convent fire, and looking at him directly, I said: "I know nothing, Papa."

He said: "Call Hugo to come here immediately." Hugo was found. "Qui, qui a fait ça, hein?" asked my father again, now in a very rich new dressing gown.

"I know nothing, Papa," said Hugo.

Some servants were called, and the Killer—but nobody knew anything. Papa sent the servants out and then said:

"Now then, nobody has the courage to say, 'I did it'— to tell the truth—" *paff paff*, and *paff paff*—we each had two smacks on the face, and as we turned, we got kicks in our backsides until we reached the door.

"That is not all," said Papa. "You will hear from me tomorrow, at the office at eight."

Sometimes, when he became furious, he would pick up the stick or a whip and would come after us. We saved ourselves by running in different directions.

In one of the wine caves in the rocky basement I found my brother with Hitler—my brother was drinking—and then we went for a walk. It was getting dark and the fireworks were being prepared. Everywhere people stood in clusters in the dark, and lined the roads, and stood silhouetted on hills, waiting for the show to start. It was a wonderful night for a celebration. The band was arriving. They were in gala uniforms. The castle was bathed in floodlights and, below, the Moselle was flowing silently.

I dressed quickly and went downstairs. Now there was soft music, and Papa, in a dress uniform, the best-looking man in the place. Oh and now Papa was in his element— and that was something we would never forgive him. At soirees, with people, with women, he was the charmer, intelligent, witty, full of stories, not at all political, or military, or a ramrod General. He danced, laughed, talked —had every woman in love with him—and told stories that were funny and intelligent dirty ones that were sometimes very profound. Only when he faced us children did the iron mask of authority go over his face—the same that he showed to the soldiers in the caserne—and now, he changed his face again and called my name sharply.

The reception was under way. Everybody was there, including an announcer at the receiving line. As I passed my father, he snapped an order at me: "Get me my cigarette case," and, to let him know that in my eyes he was no better now than he had been before, I answered as I always did when he snapped at me: "Oui, mon Colonel," and ran upstairs to get him his golden and tasseled cigarette case with his perfumed cigarettes. On the way down I thought I heard a cowbell ring. Hugo came out of the Trinkstube. He was very drunk. From the thousand and one objects that decorated this room he had taken a huge cowbell and hung it around his neck—on his head was an ancient wooden mask with feathers. He had on a military tunic and the trousers of his pajamas were tucked into riding boots. And pinned to his chest were all of Papa's medals—the large ones which were never worn, but only the ribbons thereof. In this wild get-up he was rushing like a madman down the main staircase into the salon where all the guests were. The Killer caught him in time and dragged him out.

At supper, Colonel de Voltera and his wife were seated at table with my parents, and the Killer, who served them, reported that Papa played the martyr father again and told Colonel de Voltera that his children would be the death of him.

10. THE DEATH OF VERONIQUE

IT IS IN THE NATURE of the military man, and especially one who gets as far as General, to see things through—and so Papa decided that somehow he would bring Frau Lampe into line—as he tried with us—correct the demoralization that had taken the place of discipline in her kitchen, and make it work properly.

The occasion of this new attack on the kitchen was a luncheon he had to give, to celebrate the anniversary of the regiment. At first it was to be a dinner and dance, but in view of the difficulties of such an undertaking, Papa changed it to a luncheon for a hundred and twenty officers and their wives.

That he thought Frau Lampe, or rather he, could handle.

He made up the menu beforehand. Her beloved Ochsenmaulsalat had been modified into an aspic. Then there would be something she was sure to be able to make: quenelles de brochet. There weren't any remarkable fish in the Moselle except the pike. Pike, on account of its

dry, flaky flesh, is made into dumplings and served with a
sauce. It is one of the most liked dishes in the French
kitchen. After that there would be roast chicken, salad, and
ice cream. There was no danger in any of these dishes.
He asked for Frau Lampe. She came in, she was hot, her
face looked like a lacquered duck—the plum and egg
curves had gone out of it. Papa attempted to charm her
and offered her a seat with his most elegant gesture. He
asked me to read the menu to her, and she said, Tya, she
could do all that but what was the fish dish like? That was
what he wanted to talk to her about. The pike was the
most common fish caught in the waters of the Moselle. It
was also a common fish in France, but it was not the most
delicate of fishes. There was, however, a time-honored,
simple recipe in the French kitchen, and he thought that it
might be added to the cookbook of Frau Lampe and enrich
her cuisine.

"Tya—fish cakes and fish balls I know how to make,"
said Frau Lampe with lightning flashes around the eyes.

"Oui oui, Madame, d'accord," said Papa. "Fish cakes
and fish balls are very good and they are appreciated in
France. However, these are a sort of glorified fish ball—
very good—extremely delicate in taste and easy to make.
I have had it written down for you, Madame Lampe, in
German." Papa picked up the recipe and gave it to Frau
Lampe, who read it with great suspicion as if someone had
handed her an outrageous bill for something she had never
bought.

"In a mortar pound the flesh of the pike, adding one-
half pound of frangipane."

"What is frangipane?"

I translated: "It's made of flour, yolks of eggs, salt, pepper, nutmeg, and melted butter and diluted over boiled
milk. You stir and boil, and then let it cool, and add it to
the fish meat; now you work the mortar thoroughly to
make the fish combine with beef marrow, then you put it
into the refrigerator. When you cook the quenelles, you
make elongated balls of the stuff you have in the mortar,
with your hands covered with flour and on a flour-covered
board—"

Now Frau Lampe exploded: "Tya Tya, all that is very
schön und gut, and you don't have to explain to me—
or show me how I should make it—I know how to make it,
I am a cook—it's like marrow dumplings, except with
pike—but for these fish balls we need pike, and there is
no pike."

I translated this to my father.

He asked: "But all these fishermen, and the fishboxes in
the Moselle—what are they doing?"

"There is no pike, Your Excellency Herr General," said
Frau Lampe, "and you want to know why? Because your
soldiers steal them all—they break open the fishboxes at
night, and what they don't steal swims away. On the black
market perhaps you can get all the pike you want—I think
your soldiers can tell you where. But a decent German
Hausfrau cannot buy any pike anywhere, so if you get
the pike for me, I will make you those dumplings, and
now may I go?"

Frau Lampe went back down into her kitchen and
knocked about with her pots and pans and screamed at her
help.

Papa, with his usual thoroughness, went to investigate

the absence of pike. Frau Lampe had told him the truth. We knew all about it, for we were down on the river a great deal.

Veronique often rowed in her skiff and went up as far as the castle, sometimes tying her boat to the pier there, and then joining us at the tower for a meal. Afterward Hugo would go down with her and help her into her boat, and she would drift back down. Sometimes we went with her. It was a lovely ride, the castle lay still, reflected in the water, and there was only the sound of the waves, and then quiet until the trains passed. These came frequently and they would appear out of a tunnel under the castle, lying sideways as they went along the curve of the Moselle, and for two miles their lighted windows would be reflected in the water. Then, as they turned the curve, the trains would lean over to one side and clatter over some switches, and some went along the left bank of the river and others turned right, over the stone bridge, and went into the city. Near the stone bridge were a few whirlpools, and there one had to be careful not to crash against the stone pillars. After passing under the bridge, at the right bank of the river, one could see the house occupied by Colonel de Voltera and there Veronique tied up her boat at the end of the ride. She was a good swimmer and there was no danger in any of this.

Veronique often went on the river alone at night, especially in moonlight. She had more freedom than I; she wore her hair short and those trousers I envied so much and her brother's large sweaters. I would have liked to dress like that but it would have meant endless scandal at home. As long as I lived at Hohenlinden I had to appear properly dressed, as they called it, in skirts and blouses, and a hat. My mother still decided on my clothes, which I hated.

On Saturday and Sunday we stayed away from the Silvery Pike and the Moselle, as hundreds of soldiers of the various armies of occupation strolled along the riverbank in the hope of picking up German girls—they were quite open about it. Others went boating and still others amused themselves late at night by breaking open the fishboxes and letting the pike loose. The trouble had started with the soldiers, although military police were all about.

Our own soldiers soon found out that the pike brought a high price, mostly because the French wives and their cooks bought them for the officers' kitchens. The shortage drove the price up higher. There started a nightly raiding of the fishboxes. The German fishermen were unable to stop this thieving and the German police had nothing to say. The fishermen, not being allowed out of their houses at night, finally appealed to the French authorities, who issued orders that anyone caught robbing the viviers would be punished. But nothing was done about it. In those days there were dozens of such orders and nobody paid attention to them. There developed a riverfront war in which a German was drowned and several French badly hurt.

It was during this time that Papa had the idea of having Frau Lampe make quenelles de brochet, and he investigated the conditions on the river for himself. He asked Colonel de Voltera to take stern measures. There was a new order forbidding all boating on the Moselle after dark, and to enforce it guards were posted along both sides of the river. The guards were partial to our troops and the situation went from bad to worse. Guards on land were powerless—the stealing of pike was mostly done from boats. Colonel de Voltera took personal charge of the situation and issued orders that the sentries should shoot at anyone not rowing to shore after proper warning, and that all, regardless of rank, German and French alike, were to be arrested by the military police. These warnings were posted.

One night Veronique took the rowboat and, after drifting down the Moselle, turned the boat and rowed against the stream, coming close to the bridge. There was a warning shouted, but it was drowned out by the noise of a train passing over the bridge; then a single shot was fired, and with one bullet she was killed.

It was hazy on the river. The boat, in which she was alone, drifted under the bridge and down the river, and it came to the place where the Moselle turns in a wide arc, and there it bumped against the fishboxes and came to rest near the Silvery Pike.

The Germans, scared, were nowhere to be seen. Only the woman who kept the tavern went down to the river, and she recognized Veronique and had enough courage to call us. Veronique lay peaceful, as if she were posing and faking sleep and would jump up any minute; one arm was outside the boat in the water—from there, her father lifted her into his car. It was the first time I had ever seen someone dead, and it did not scare me. I only wished I had been in her place.

Martial law was declared once more, and my father ordered a complete and thorough inquiry which almost drove several people insane. It was established that the shot fired came from a French army rifle, and eventually it became clear that one of the sentries stationed at the

Moselle Bridge had fired the shot. He had acted according to orders. The poor man was in a terrible state. He swore that he had shouted "halt" three times, and that the occupant of the boat, whom he took for a German, had paid no attention. He had then wanted to fire a warning shot and not hurt anyone; he had pointed the rifle in the direction of the boat and aimed ahead of it about five feet, and had hit her by the dreadful coincidence of his own bad aim and the boat's movement in the six-mile speed of the river's flow. It was dusk, he did not hear anything, the boat drifted on; he shouted to the next sentry, who let the boat pass out from under the bridge, and then it began to twist and turn in the whirlpools and he did not want to waste ammunition on it—since he was not sure whether it was one of our soldiers or a German.

On such details hangs life, and now there was the unhappy father. He had not discussed the orders at table—which might have warned her—they had had pike on the day of the tragedy—all these things form a bitter mosaic.

In the church below the castle, whose bells we heard day and night, Veronique was given a quiet service. In a white little-girl batiste dress, with flowers on her chest and a silver cross in her hands and the rosary wound around them, Veronique lay at the house for a day, pouting in protest, in a casket that was like the fishboxes in the Moselle. Her mother went with the body to France to inter her in Beaufort.

My mother and father were shocked and unhappy. I was forbidden to go near the Moselle and Papa, looking down on the river at dusk with Mama standing by, said that now perhaps I saw how right they were in asking me to dress properly. If poor Veronique had been in a white blouse, for instance, and a skirt, she would be alive today. I said that if Papa hadn't ordered Frau Lampe to make quenelles de brochet, Veronique would be alive today also, and if fathers talked to their children she would be alive too—because she would have been warned. And I said I would give anything to be in her place.

Worse than the soldier who had shot Veronique, and who now looked like a madman, was her brother Alain. He seemed to have no hands, no feet, no eyes. He did not blame the soldier, he did not blame Veronique, instead he blamed the Germans and our awful parents.

He turned these things over and over in his mind. I stroked his hair and let him talk. I said that of course Veronique was killed the moment she was hit, the shot went through her heart and she had not suffered. Alain swore that he would revenge her. He said that if ever any German molested me, he would kill him. I was his only hope and he would give me the love he had had for his sister.

The Killer reported to Alain that Reinhild had discussed the case with someone on the telephone and had said: "How can you expect things to go otherwise with girls who smoke on the street and go to taverns at night. And what a piece of luck it is for the Germans that a Frenchman shot her."

11. THE GERMAN LESSON

MY FATHER INSISTED that I take German lessons, and twice a week I went to a house where a Madame Kwikert, a very nice old German lady, with a pince-nez, taught me. She wore black dresses—or I should say one black dress—and high-buttoned shoes. She had a little dog who liked me. We sat in a salon with dreadful furniture, a kind of tortured dark-stained wood of no identifiable period; it looked like choir stalls. It was ugly but very respectable. There was a picture of Monsieur and Madame Kwikert—one seated and the other standing—there were vases without flowers, and although the windows were open the place always smelled of stale cooking.

Madame Kwikert was a contented and very proper little lady, who spoke faultless German-school French; that is, she never made a grammatical mistake, or one in pronunciation. When she talked one could hear how seriously she had taken her lessons so long ago. She straightened out the cloth on the table and quoted phrases from German poetry, and then the lesson began—was ist das—das ist ein

Fenster—das ist eine Türe. Schön gut, Mademoiselle. She was kindness itself and never impatient. I returned from her house carrying a brief case in which I had my lessons. I went from her house across the Amalienstrasse and through a park, then to the Paradeplatz and the armory, where I waited for the car to take me to Hohenlinden.

One day, after I had finished the lessons and was walking in the park, a German boy whom I had not seen approach overtook me, and with a brusque gesture tore my brief case out of my hand and threw it into the bushes. It was late afternoon, and as if he had sprung out of the earth Alain was suddenly beside me. He had a stick in his hand and he chased after the German boy. The boy ran as fast as he could, Alain after him and overtaking him.

Alain poked the stick at the German boy's chest and motioning to a tree in the park he said: "Go there and tear off a stick like this." It was a thin, flexible stick. The boy went and did as he was told; he took it from the tree which Alain had indicated and he broke it off equal in size to the other. The German boy had fawn-colored leather shorts, and at the bottom of them an inch of underwear was visible; he had nude legs, and wore short socks and brown low-cut shoes, his sleeves rolled up and leather suspenders. He seemed a nice boy and of a good family. I felt sick. In back of me there was a statue of Schiller with eyeless eyes and long hair. It had a Latin inscription and was of very old, discolored white marble. It was on a huge socle of granite, mossy and dark gray, and here on a sandy enclosure around the statue they started. I sank down on a bench there, praying for this to end—somehow—quickly.

They were equal in size and they went at each other with fury, across the face, across the legs, across the arms, across the body. Alain had only one advantage—he had long trousers and the sleeves of his shirt were down. When I had arrived at the park, there were nursemaids and elderly people on the benches, and children playing—the population of a park on a nice afternoon. Now they had all disappeared. Some people passed on the paths, but no one interfered. They could see that it was a German boy fighting with a French boy and they looked the other way. It lasted a long time—perhaps five, perhaps ten minutes; they fought on every side of the statue, and the German was crying with fury, his arms and legs were bloody; Alain was bleeding from nose and mouth. There was a policeman who seemed to see nothing either—but he watched from a distant tree and was writing in a book, and when the German saw this, he cried "stop" and indicated that they would continue some other place, and they both ran.

I ran after them. I was half scared, half fascinated by the fight. It was awful. I felt as I had that long time ago at the bullfight, but here somehow I admired both of them and suddenly when I saw that in a way they played it fairly, I had much curiosity about how it would end—it was like watching the fire. I hoped that both would win. Alain led the way; they ran out of the park and through the street toward the armory, where our soldiers stood guard. There, near the bandstand, they started again. Our soldiers massed inside the gates of the armory and shouted encouragement to Alain, and they cried things like: "Kill the German bastard." The German boy began to collapse with fatigue and he got wobbly and then Alain left him alone.

We walked into the armory and Alain washed himself. There remained from this fight a scar, glowing red, under his right eye. I was very proud of it and would have followed it with my finger if he had let me. The brief case was delivered at the castle that night. I dreamed of the German boy. I saw him like Joan of Arc—being led to the stake—and the boughs with which the fire was built were all sticks like the one they had battled with. I awoke and cried in terror, but again there was no answer from the next room. I only heard Reinhild move in her bed and knew she was awake.

12. THE INQUISITION

WE HAD A SECRET RENDEZVOUS at the tower one day. There were the peculiar green-tinted glasses that are called Römer, and Alain filled one for me, and then he said:

"We have been thinking and thinking for weeks now about why that German snatched your brief case from you —certainly not to get your German lessons. Was everything in it when you got it back?"

"Yes, everything was in it."

"But there could have been something placed in it, which was taken out while the brief case lay there. Did you see anything? Anybody?"

"No, I was absorbed in watching the fight."

"Now, for example, couldn't Reinhild have taken something from your father's desk and put it into your brief case. Do you follow me, something like the notes you took on his conversation with General von der Linde. During the German lesson did you unpack the brief case?"

"I did not, except to take out the papers on which I was working."

"Now, if one had parents like everybody else's, we could go to my father, or to yours, and say: 'Is there anything missing among your classified papers?' and there would be some co-operation. But not with us. We would be told to run along and mind our own business.

"This battle with the German boy was no accident—they don't do anything, the Germans, from the day they are born, that has not got a good reason behind it. I hate Reinhild as much as you do and I suspect the worst.

"We have to find out what's behind it. This Hitler business is all a clever masquerade—not that she isn't a fanatical Nazi, but the openness with which she admits it is to throw us off the scent."

I had terrible nightmares, always, but now they increased, and as brave as I showed myself during the day I was afraid at night. I awoke in bed, covered with cold sweat. I was drawn to the window—I was afraid the ceiling would come down on me. At other times, I was afraid to move—and one night there came again a moment of hysteria when I could no longer bear it and I cried out: "Reinhild, come—come and stay with me, please—Reinhild, come—help me." I heard her move in her bed next door, but she never came.

Hugo and Alain found out that there was a gang of young people in Weimarein, to which the young man belonged, and also a girl. Her name was Sieglinde. For a few days they studied the movements of the gang. They all worked after school hours and they saw that Sieglinde was with them regularly, and toward dusk she and the boy bicycled home together. She lived in the Villenviertel, as the quarter of the best houses of the bourgeoisie is called.

It was beyond the castle at the foot of the hill on which the tower stood.

They discovered that the girl had been with the boy that day. The soldiers on guard had seen her go to him after the fight. She had a bicycle which she had pushed along as she walked away with him.

"Something has to be done," said Alain. "Let's not waste any more time with watching them." They now dressed themselves in raincoats and pulled down their hats, to look like detectives and older, and they rode around with the Killer in his jeep. One day toward dusk, when they cruised in the Villenviertel, they saw Sieglinde on her bicycle coming toward them. They stopped her and told her to get into the jeep, and that she was wanted for questioning.

They drove her up to the old tower and locked her in the prison cellar, and then they debated and sat close together while I made myself a sandwich and some coffee. They brought her up and questioned her. She did not answer them with anything but her name and address. She had known about the attack of the boy on me—it was her brother. She said that he was only a boy and that he had been absolutely right. French soldiers had come to the house that morning and requisitioned some rugs and a typewriter, and he was angry and said that now he would steal something in return. She had dared him and he had said, "I'll show you—see that girl there"—and had run and taken the brief case. "Very understandable, no?" She had dismissed it from her mind—one always was in some kind of trouble these days. Had they belonged to the Hitler Jungend? Of course they had, everybody had—how could you have gone to school? Or done anything? What was she doing now? She was now helping out in a rental library. My brother said that rental libraries were the classic place for the receiving and sending of information.

"Are you or your brother connected with the underground?"

She was a pretty girl and she laughed and said that these were ridiculous questions and to let her go, as her parents and her brother would be worried that something had happened to her.

"Not yet," said Alain. They put her back into the prison cellar and then they sat down together again and plotted. They got a blowtorch and some rope, and in the shed found branding irons to mark the wine barrels with. They arranged all this, lit the torch, and told me to ice more wine as this might take a long time. Then they arranged the table, took everything off it, closed the curtains, and left only the glaring light, and Alain went down to get the girl.

Alain said to her that she had the choice of telling the truth, or else things would go very badly with her. He told her that he hated the methods of persuasion they were about to use on her, but had no choice. She was pale, scared, and she said that she had nothing to tell them. They lifted her on the table, turned her face down, and tied her legs and arms to the four corners. She did not resist. Alain took the branding iron and heated it glowing red in front of her. She still said that she had nothing to say.

"I wish you would," he said, "for you are a pretty girl, and I hate to disfigure you for life."

The Killer said, "Not the face—let's start on her back."

The Killer then took a red velvet pillow from a chair and held her head on it, and Alain zipped open her dress in back, and while Hugo pressed the red-hot iron on a pork chop and made it sizzle and smell like burned flesh, Alain placed a piece of ice on her bare back. She cried out in terrible agony, as if her flesh had really been seared, and she said:

"I'll tell, I'll tell you everything I know."

"Good," said Alain. Alain put the branding iron into a bucket of water, where it made a hissing sound, and he asked the Killer to bring him the first-aid kit from the jeep. He applied some burn ointment to her back, and a compress, and attached this with adhesive tape. She screamed whenever he touched her, for she was certain she had been badly burned.

They allowed her to sit up, and she looked like a ghastly half-demented person. She sobbed and said: "Believe me, I can't tell you much, for I am not in the inner confidences; they keep the very important things to themselves. I am only vaguely familiar with what it is, and what goes on."

"Tell us what you know," said Alain.

"How shall I begin?"

"What is the organization known as?"

"They are the Werewolves."

"Do they have some kind of rules?"

"Yes, a very thorough instructions manual."

"And what does it say?"

"The main orders are patience and organization. Time, we are told, works for us. Observe the enemy and make a close study of his habits and peculiarities. There I was of use."

"Who is the enemy?"

"You—the Allies—and above all the Germans that side with you."

"Yes—go on, please—what else?"

"We recruit members—we divide the people of the town into various classes."

"What are they?"

"Those who will make good Werewolves." She lowered her head and mumbled ashamedly.

"Then there are those that are not to be trusted, then those who remain passive, and the last, and those you mark well, the ones that have gone over to the enemy."

"Do you have the list of names of those?"

"No, I'm not that important."

The Killer offered her a cigarette. They gave her some wine and she smoked.

"Now go on, tell us what you do, having selected the people who make good Werewolves?"

"Now you instruct people in how to behave so as not to arouse suspicion. How to hide people, how to help others escape. You organize sabotage, you mark those who will be burned."

"Ah, at last."

The room still smelled of burned flesh, and it was filled with smoke; and they sitting together, and the frightened girl and the light shining on her—all that was exciting.

"C'est vachement sensas," said Hugo to the Killer.

The Killer said that the girl was vachement sympat.

"Now then, Mademoiselle," said Alain, "having told us how the Werewolves are selected, will you tell us a little of what their immediate plans are?"

She said she did not know.

She had pushed her blond hair back and stopped sobbing. She wiped tears from her cheeks, she was very well built, had good legs, and she looked at Alain pleadingly with her large forget-me-not eyes.

Alain said: "Would you give us the names of the gang?"

"Please don't ask me that."

"No," said Hugo, "that wouldn't be fair."

"Very well," said Hugo, "we have other means of finding out."

They held a whispered conference, and then Alain said that they would let her go if she gave them other information instead. She sighed and said that she didn't know anything more than she had told.

Alain asked, "Surely there is something about the Werewolves, a run-down on their methods of working, on their training and instruction?"

"Yes," she said, "that I think I can tell. They have a training manual on how to behave, for example, if you get in a skirmish with the enemy, especially the military police when several go at you at the same time. You must remain in the center of the room for that way they can all hit you."

My brother said: "That's fine advice—you mean you must *not*—"

"Yes, that is what I said, didn't I?"

"No, you said you must remain in the center. Well, Mademoiselle, you are a little confused. Take another glass of wine and a cigarette, and tell us why you must *not* remain in the center of the room."

"You must not remain in the center of the room, for

that way they can all hit you at the same time. You must try and get away into a corner and not try and be a hero. Then only two or three can hit you."

"Very good advice," said the Killer.

"When outnumbered, be smart. The next thing to remember is not to try and remain upright—you gain nothing. Act as if you were unconscious, let yourself fall to the floor, play dead or critically hurt. It is very important to roll on your abdomen—you also pull in your chin, let your ribs protect the most sensitive organs, loosen your bones, and keep your elbows at the sides of the body to ward off kicks against your kidneys."

Alain was taking notes. Hugo asked if there was anything to add, just a little more, and then they would drive her home and let her go.

There were instructions which to her shame she had tried to follow but miserably failed in.

"That is, one must hold before oneself that there are things to bear, solitary confinement in dark cells, being locked into standing coffins, being in a box where you cannot sit or lie down, getting teeth knocked out, being left freezing, getting toes and fingernails pulled out, being kept without sleep for nights, being burned, being damaged by electricity, and being morally smashed. That, meine Herren," said Sieglinde, "is what you have done to me. Now may I go? I have nothing more to tell."

Alain said: "Just one more question. For example, what does sabotage consist of?"

"Oh, spoiling things, making things not work, interference with communications."

"Could you be more specific? Tell me of a certain objective."

"Well, let's say the derailment of trains is very important."

"Is anything like that planned now, as far as you know?"

She said, "If it is, I wouldn't be told," and she looked so honestly and directly at Alain that he said that the interview was ended.

The Killer had thrown the piece of meat that had served in this scene of torture in the garbage can. He was busy making sandwiches, and the German girl couldn't take her eyes from the knife, the bread, the ham, and the butter. "Would you like something to eat?" said the Killer.

"Ja ja, bitte schön," she said.

He gave her a sandwich, and she ate it in three bites, and swallowed hard and it was gone.

"She's hungry," said Hugo. "Give her another." He asked what she would like.

"Oh anything," she said. She would like to have an egg —she had not had an egg for a long time—so they fried her some eggs, and she began to tell what their life had been, and how wonderful this white bread in thick slices with butter was. They had eaten dry black bread, they had eaten garbage. She looked at the can and said could she take what was in it along?

"Have you a dog at home?"

"Nein nein," she said, "for my parents," and she was in the garbage can with both hands and expertly fished out everything eatable. She commented on the wunderbare cutlet. We made a package of food for her. She thanked us with embarrassment and then Alain and Hugo put on their raincoats and pulled down their hats, and with cigarettes glowing they went out into the dark and started the jeep. Her bicycle was in the jeep, but it was late now and the sentries stopped people. So Alain and Hugo took her to the staff car. It was agreed that she wouldn't say anything to anyone, and that the secret of the visit would be kept at the castle, and that would leave everyone honorable. "In fact," said Alain, "you have not told us anything really important." They drove Sieglinde to a street close to her house and let her go.

The Killer cleaned up the pantry and put the instruments of torture and the ropes away. Alain and Hugo came back and were full of themselves and their counter-Werewolf work. They discussed the girl and her beauty, her legs, her back, her hair, her eyes—vachement sympat—and, of course, the fact that she had not given away the members of the gang was noble. I said that, after all, they had not pressed her very much. It looked as if the three had fallen in love with her, which often happens between French and Germans, and not only straight love but also hate love.

I asked them if they had her telephone number. Yes, they did, and her friends called her "Dotty" because her real name was Dorothea; she had become Sieglinde in the BDM, the League of German Girls.

13. ARE YOU HUNGRY

ARE YOU COLD

PAPA WAS AWAY on a tour of inspection. When he came back, Hugo decided to tell him about the Werewolves.

When one sought an audience with the General, one had to be properly dressed, for first came the inspection of the person before him, from head to foot. Hugo adjusted his tie; he had his notes in his pocket and, since this was the first time he would really talk to his father as man to man on serious business, he went over very carefully what he would say to him. I advised him not to go. But he said that it was important and even if it were difficult he had to risk it. He made the appointment and at the proper time knocked on the door of Papa's office. As he was admitted, he saw that Reinhild was with Papa. She left the room. Papa looked at Hugo, who went toward him and started eagerly:

"Papa—I have—" and then *paff paff* and *paff paff*—he had four smacks in the face.

"I will tell you what you have," screamed Papa. "You

have a disgusting character and I am putting you under house arrest for a month. You are not to leave the grounds without my permission. The same goes for Alain." Papa then screamed himself into red-faced anger; he knew all about the shocking happenings. It had all been reported to him that Alain and Hugo had picked up a girl of good family, taken her to a hide-out, and undressed her there, and what went on after that could be imagined. There were other means of satisfying one's lowest instincts—there were places—and girls—for that.

If one of the soldiers had committed such an offense he would be court-martialed. For the sons of the commanding officers to do a thing that was inadmissible! "Sapristi! Have you no shame, no honor? Nom de nom!"—he went into one of his set pieces and when Hugo said: "Please let me explain," he screamed: "I have said what I have said—I have nothing more to say. Now—get out of my sight." When it came to that point it was better to save oneself, but Hugo remained and said:

"Papa, you must listen to me."

Papa picked up his stick and said: "Now go, or I'll lose my temper."

Hugo came out. He looked, young as he was, as if he had suffered a stroke. He said: "It's Reinhild. Papa always listens to whoever talks to him first. She has told him." Alain called her "La Guenon," which means the female gorilla.

"She's dangerous—she has to go. We will make life so awful for her that she will have to leave." We looked for Reinhild—she was in the garden walking up and down.

Alain came over; he had not yet seen his father. Hugo told him what had happened. We were near the gardenhouse where we had thrown knives before. The knives were in a box in the gardenhouse. Alain got the box with the knives. Reinhild was about to enter the gardenhouse—she had the handle of the door in her hand. Alain called her name sharply—and she turned. He had his mad green eyes on her and he said to Hugo: "Here, you are better at this," and handed him the box. Reinhild stood flat against the door. Alain said: "Go on, Hugo"—and Hugo took the knives and started to throw. They went very close and, as Hugo threw them, Alain said with each throw:

"Dirty cow, get out of this house."

"You German bitch,"

"We know your game."

"If you don't go, you'll be sorry."

"Things will go badly with you."

"We are not fooling."

"Go and pack now."

"Move out with your filthy business."

"Guenon, canaille, ordure—"

She stood there, looking straight at Alain, and she did not blink. The knives were all in the wood.

She said: "Are you through?" Without another word she walked away.

"She's tough," said Alain. "We must think of something else. We must get rid of her, and another thing we must do, we must prove to your father that there is really danger."

"He'll never listen to us."

"I think I have a way," said Alain, "to make them all listen. You know what she said, the girl, about what they did—sabotage, destroying communications, and derailing trains. It's very simple, and with that we will get rid of

Reinhild. We will inform your father through official channels, in writing, that there is a plot to derail the express from Düsseldorf. We will then derail it ourselves. That is all—I know how it is done, it isn't hard at all."

"But that will kill people."

"Not necessarily—we'll derail it after the tunnel on the curve as it comes into the station. It slows down there. It will make a lot of trouble and that is precisely what we want. We will write a letter and give them the time and the place, and we will be rid of her and will have done something." Alain and Hugo had at one time cut themselves and each had touched the other with his blood, and one had to do what the other did.

"I'll do it," said Hugo, "and I don't care how it ends."

They went to the tower and plotted there, and when it got dark Hugo went to his room and turned out the light, and an hour later he climbed out the window and went into the town with Alain to study the problem of derailing the train.

During this time I felt as if I were going to become ill from anxiety and break down. I could hardly walk, I did not sleep. I thought of all the things that might happen: that Alain or Hugo would get under the train and lose a leg, or get killed—or that the Werewolves would kill them. They went to town every night, crossing over fields, walking in shadows and side streets. I was grateful that the derailment presented all kinds of obstacles and that they could not immediately carry it out.

I tried to persuade them that it was all like children playing with fire, and I said most certainly Papa had people who knew all these things—and were there to watch out.

Almost every day some Germans were arrested, mostly

youths, and they were made to talk. And Reinhild was perhaps just a stupid woman with a German sense of duty. I tried again to talk to Reinhild, but as always she did not answer when I called her, she just moved in her bed. I prayed, I went to church, I wanted to talk to my father but that was impossible. Alain and Hugo talked of nothing but derailment. They measured the rails, watched trains come, calculated the speeds, and in the tower they built a model of the station to scale.

There was street fighting at night, but so far Alain and Hugo and the Killer always got away, chiefly because the Killer carried three guns, and Hitler was along.

Finally they wrote the letter. I said to them to come to reason, and that they risked their lives. If they were caught they would be tried and be locked up, for years perhaps.

Hugo said: "Oh, what of it. When one has parents like we have—one is fated to be monstrous and end badly."

The train was derailed the night after they had written the letter. Nobody was hurt. The locomotive and a baggage car had jumped the rails, the engineer had suffered some minor hurts, a few people were bruised. The next day all suspicious Germans were arrested. Papa and Colonel de Voltera canceled the house arrests of their sons. It was impossible for Papa ever to praise any of us. He merely grunted something. He shook hands with Alain and Hugo and when all had been explained to him, he said: "Continuez." That is always the way with parents who think that after years of maltreatment and misery they can wipe the slate clean with a grudging "sorry." It's like people who are innocent and who have been put in jail and then are let out with an apology by the judge, but it doesn't give back the lost time, or take away the agony they have suffered. That is the way we thought as we were celebrating the success of the undertaking. Reinhild stayed on. "Now," said Alain to the Killer and to Hugo, "while we are personae gratae, and there is a favorable climate, let's put our heads together seriously and find a way to get rid of the German Guenon once and for all."

This problem they had settled in several ways. They would wait for the weekend when Papa and Mama went away.

It was the time when one could requisition anything—there was no one who had not something or other that he had seen, wanted, or taken from the Germans. The deaf chauffeur had requisitioned six alarm clocks, all of which he wound every night in the hope that ringing in concert they would wake him up.

Alain asked me if I had seen any toy stores in town, and any dolls in them. The toy stores were pitifully empty. He said they needed dolls, many of them. They went to several toy shops but found none. Those they saw were of wood or porcelain and that did not help them. They needed dolls made of celluloid. They plotted again and then the Killer got into his jeep and they put on their slouch hats and they said they would requisition some celluloid dolls from children. I said to Hugo and Alain and the Killer: "Don't do it, please. How can you—what have little children to do with war—what have they done to you?"

"You lack understanding," said Alain. "We take dolls from them, and that's too bad. Well they took fathers, mothers, sisters from our children—and these bastards will all grow up and be Germans and do it again and again

and again—and I'm for killing the lot. If you need anything to excuse it, remember the village of St. Roch. Remember where they locked women and children in the
church, and then set it on fire. Don't ever talk to me about
kindness to Germans."

They went from house to house and they collected a
great many dolls. Sometimes the Germans hid things but
none of them suspected that the French would requisition
dolls from their little girls—so it was easy.

They waited until our parents had gone for the weekend to Baden-Baden.

In Reinhild's room stood the large carved closet of dark-
stained wood, some eight feet wide and six feet high. They
filled this with the celluloid dolls and closed it. Then they
got the key to my room, and locked the door from the inside
and climbed out my bathroom window. Reinhild came
into her room, and they locked her door from the outside.
Then they touched two wires, and a moment after, the
exploding started. The door of the closet burst open and
the dolls' arms and legs and heads shot through the room
like a rain of fire. The room filled with acrid smoke. After
the explosion in the room, Reinhild banged on the door
and begged to be let out. The closet was burning and there
was smoke thick as milk; choking and crying she came out.
Alain took her by the throat and said that if she repeated
anything, said a word to anyone, she would be killed. She
didn't say anything.

She was, without her normal hauteur, an old, sick-looking
woman. She had never said anything, she told Alain; she
knew what we thought and that we suspected her, but she
had never reported anything to my father. Most probably
he got the information from the police or the parents of

Sieglinde or out of some anonymous letter—things are talked about—there are people who carry stories false and true.

She said that she needed the position and that she knew we all hated her and that she had no reason to love us, either.

In a sobbing breakdown she fell on a couch in the hall. We put her in a guest room. Hugo and I had thrown water on the burning closet. The fire was blamed on faulty wiring.

In the next week, Reinhild had recovered from her fright and gradually there was a return to her old personality. She looked ten years older and tired, but suddenly her regimen was as strict as it had been before. I got very hungry sometimes, during the day or afternoon, and I asked for something to eat. She never allowed it. "No eating between meals," she always said, and now she said it again, and I had to run to the tower to get something to eat.

On the Fourteenth of July, the French in residence in Germany celebrated the national holiday. There were fireworks on the Moselle and all the military pomp that could be unwound, like at Papa's promotion.

While a battalion of paratroopers marched past fifty feet away, with their band blaring, in an adjoining side street Alain and Hugo were set upon by the gang of Werewolves. When they got through with them, they were left for dead in the street.

After the celebration was over, some Germans going home found them and called the police. In the hospital they were identified.

They had lost because the Killer that night was on duty

with my father, who reviewed the troops at the torchlight parade. Also Hitler was not with them.

Alain and Hugo were transferred to the French military hospital and were there for three weeks.

It took the German police a month and ten days to find who had derailed the Düsseldorf express. When they discovered it, they handled it as all such matters were handled in those days. General von der Linde came for another Kriegspiel. They talked, a bottle of the best wine of the house was opened, cigars were smoked, and then the General stated what the real purpose of his visit was.

He put the dossier of the German police into Papa's hands and there was the story. The police held back, and the whole thing would be hushed up of course, since we were technically still at war and they had no police power and, of course, on account of Papa's position.

The German General said that we were living in unhappy times. He thanked him for the wine, excused himself for bringing bad news, clicked his heels, and left.

This was followed by a horrible scene in our house between father and son, and one even more so in the house of Colonel de Voltera, who went to punish his son, and Alain said to him:

"Don't raise your hand against me. I know of what I am capable, and I know my own strength. I am no longer a child, and if you touch me I will forget that you are my father."

Colonel de Voltera got on the phone to speak to my father and they then called the provost marshal and had both Alain and Hugo put into a cell at the stockade. That night Alain and Hugo each wrote a letter to their parents, not asking for forgiveness—but that they be allowed to leave to join the army and go overseas to fight in Indo-China—they said that they had to do something to prove themselves. They would only bring disgrace on their families if they stayed in Germany. They had to have danger, they had to be men, they had to be treated as such and not as children.

The letters were read by the parents, who met and agreed that this was the best solution for everyone, and the requests were granted. They were old enough and strong enough, and Papa was influential enough to get them where they wanted to be.

Late in the night, after this decision had been made, Colonel de Voltera and Papa went to the stockade, and each one had his son released. Papa was a quiet, sad man. He had never been able to say anything kind to any of us, and he could again say nothing. They came back in an open car. He offered his hand to Hugo and he asked:

"Are you hungry?"

"Are you cold?"

And Hugo said that he couldn't answer because his throat contracted and was dry with emotion. It was the only time Papa had ever voiced any concern for him. Hugo just shook his head.

14. THE ASSASSINS

WHEN IT HAD BEEN DECIDED that Hugo and Alain would go to special training and eventually to Indo-China, where they said they wanted to go, and all details had been set, the parents said their good-bys to them. In this ceremony of coldness and embarrassment, which is possible only in family life, the parents were the children and I felt sorry for them all.

Colonel de Voltera and my father asked their sons for a few words of honor, promises that they would not go beyond the properly policed grounds and would leave the place only when the final orders for departure were given them and would properly follow instructions as to when and where and how they would leave.

There were two or three days left for them and our parents went for a holiday in Baden-Baden. The boys could have a party and invite their friends. My father said that the castle was theirs. In the car both Colonel de Voltera and my father sat stiffly erect, with military stupidity, not turning for a last look or wave of the hand.

Inside the Rittersaal, Alain and Hugo stood equally stiff, looking out over the Moselle. And so ended this part of life for them; childhood and youth that had been all wasted.

When the car was out of sight the two friends embraced each other and jumped in the air, and then plans were made for the celebration of their going away. It would be a sensational celebration.

The first thing, and before one could decide what wines to serve, was to decide on the menu. Frau Lampe came into the room, where my brother and Alain sat planning the party. "You sent for me?" she snapped. "Frau Lampe," said Hugo, smiling. "We are giving a party and we would like it to be a great success, and we would like to have something different in the way of food."

Frau Lampe said nothing. She waited.

"Frau Lampe," said Hugo, "we want to find out what you like to cook best. Please sit down, Frau Lampe."

"I can stand up," she said. "Tell me what you want."

"Why don't you suggest something, Frau Lampe?"

"I can make a good roast—a fish—a Kalbsnuesschen is nice—"

"Yes—that's very nice, but this is a special party."

"So you have a goose mit apples stuffed—or a duck. But first tell me how many?"

"Oh, from twelve to twenty."

"Maybe a pair of suckling pigs—and a soup to start with."

"It's hopeless," said Alain. "We'll end up with the choucroute, Schweinebraten, und Sauerkraut mit Kartoffelklosse."

Frau Lampe stabbed him with a deadly look and said:

"I have no time to waste here. Write down what you want on a piece of paper and send it to me in the kitchen, and I cook it—anything." With that she turned around and shuffled out in her pantoufled feet, slammed the door, and with her distressing voice trailing off in complaint she went back down into her kitchen.

Hugo said: "Caviar we can get from the American sector, they get it from the Russians. The Killer can get anything we want, partridge, for instance. He got some last week in the Black Forest—caviar with the drinks—then, to start, Rhine salmon smoked—that's easy—and after?"

"Roast partridge—that should not be too hard for her—after all it's only a bird."

"After that? Foie gras with salad—and a soufflé au Grand Marnier—"

They wrote it all down, and Hugo went down to the kitchen. Frau Lampe let her eyes run over the menu, and she said, without a change of expression, that it was possible and asked for the hour dinner would be served, so that the soufflé would be put in the oven at the right time. Now that that was settled, Hugo and Alain went to the wine cellar, to the part where the French wines and liqueurs were kept and they carefully selected everything they needed, from gin and whisky to champagne. Then they called for flowers for the table—it would be "vachement sensas" and a party to remember. For music Alain brought the favorite records of Veronique and her record player. They invited eleven of their friends, and I would be the hostess. We got paper guirlandes, and balloons, and paper hats, and decorated the knights in the Rittersaal. On the afternoon of the party Alain and Hugo started drinking whisky. They were very debonair when the guests arrived.

There was dancing and horseplay before dinner, then the candles were lit. The table was beautifully set with the best silver and an immense centerpiece of water lilies. We sat down and talked, and waited, and waited. And then Hugo got up and walked to the door that led to the kitchen, and he came back in a rage and said, "Come all of you and see what detains the service."

And there was nothing—and nobody. The kitchen was lit up, the pots were on the oven, empty, and there was no cook, no maid, no one—it was completely empty. I laughed, and Alain said: "What is funny about this? I invited friends for a dinner, and this is what awaits us."

Hugo echoed him: "Yes," he said, "I wish to apologize."

"No—I apologize, it's my party," said Alain.

They had all been drinking more and more and whisky was not their usual drink. They went back to the hall and poured themselves more drinks. Then Alain came to me and said: "This is your house, no?"

I said: "Yes, of course."

"Well then—get out there and cook something."

This seemed awfully funny and I laughed and said: "But I don't know how to cook anything."

He said: "You can make some eggs, and boil some potatoes, no?"

I said: "No, I don't know how."

He pushed me out into the kitchen. I can't stand to be touched. I said: "Be careful, Alain—or this will end badly."

"Oh now then," he said, "no airs, Mademoiselle—get busy."

I said: "I am not your maid or your cook, but I think if you ask your little friends there, they will most certainly be able to help out. They have better hands for it."

He was insulted about his friends and disappeared to call them to confront me with their quality. I took a bottle of champagne, twisted out its cork, and sat down on a chair, putting my feet on the kitchen table. I drank from the bottle. He came in, followed by the girls and their escorts, and he said:

"Get up."

I said: "Now please, it was very funny up to now, I thought you were joking—now get out all of you before I throw something at you." He came toward me and I threw the bottle of champagne like a club. It missed him, but hit the wall and there was a crash of dishes falling from the shelf, and with screams everybody ran out of the kitchen. Alain came toward me and he hit me with his fist. I fell backward on the floor. That is all I remember.

I awoke in my bed, with Alain kneeling beside me. He looked at me with his hard eyes—he did not apologize. He was half dressed, he kicked off his shoes and he came into my bed. He took me in his arms, and then pressed me into the pillows. Without a word, but holding me down, his teeth were in my throat without however biting me. This which was like murder, then, was also love, hurtful and frightening, but a pulse-racing ecstasy ending in beautiful unconsciousness such as death must be. He remained for hours. I heard Reinhild move in her bed, and loud enough for her to hear it I said to Alain:

"I told you this would end badly."

In the moments after, when I was in possession of my senses again, I made believe I was sleeping so as not to embarrass him with my presence. Always ashamed of emotion and the candor that love demands, he now thought himself safe. He bent over me and kissed me on the forehead and the hands, and he whispered apologies for last night. I made believe I was awakening, but when he saw me move, he looked at me for a second, his green eyes hard again, as I opened my eyes. He climbed out of the window. The morning star was over his shoulder for a moment, the curtains rustled. His strong hand was on the ledge and then he was gone, the way I suppose he had come. I reflected on the curious fact that all joy, in a fashion, came from pain.

I didn't sleep the rest of the night and neither did Reinhild, but she thought I did. She paced the floor and got in and out of her bed, lit the light and put it out—and spoke to herself in German and I hoped it was all curses and jealousy and bitter hatred.

The hour clanked from the towers, the birds began to sing, dawn glowed in the sky and in the river below, and I fell into deep and dreamless sleep.

Reinhild stood at my bed and woke me. My lips that hurt took me back to the night before. Reinhild told me that I had better hurry if I wanted to see my brother once more—he was leaving with Alain on a plane in an hour. She called a maid and told her to strip my bed of the linen, the stained witness to the night, and take it downstairs.

I told the maid to get out of the room. I slammed the door. I was alone with Reinhild and she was scared and watched me. I said:

"Wait until I'm ready to go."

I dressed in haste and kept her waiting, and as I put my gloves on, I said to her:

"Don't think that now that Alain and my brother are going, that things will go easier with you. I am your enemy

and you are mine—watch out." And I borrowed the phrase
that Alain had used on his father. "I know what I am
capable of and so do you—so pay attention, pay close attention or it will go very badly. Now get out, and this bed
sheet—hang it out the window like a flag. Show it to Papa
—do anything you wish with it, dirty filthy skin of a bitch-
wolf."

I ran down the stairs. The Killer was waiting and drove
me to the airfield. On the way I told him the story of the
dinner party. He smiled his grim, beautiful smile of white
teeth and black mustache, and he said: "Just wait, we'll
take care of them."

At the plane, Alain and Hugo—and Oh hello—Bonjour
—Guten Tag, Fräulein Sieglinde—were waiting.

Alain and Hugo had to play the brave and casual, and
they stood near their military baggage—and admired each
other.

"Now we are the real tough ones. Now we are true
assassins," they said as they were ordered aboard. Then the
plane took off. Sieglinde waved. I was hollow inside at the
sight of the departing plane; I suffered acute physical pain
in the pit of the stomach, and it lasted.

I came back to the empty castle and the only person
standing on the steps was Reinhild. She looked calm and
satisfied with herself, and I thought if these two boys are
killed it is your fault, for I have no doubt that it is you
who infests this house with evil and spying. She said good
evening. I walked past her without a word.

I was alone now. I had forgotten all about Frau Lampe
and the incident of the dinner with no food. It was late
when the Killer came and said: "Come, we have work to
do—the kitchen help is still absent—if you want anything

to eat, you will have to cook it yourself. They'll only come back tomorrow, when the General returns. So we will prepare a little surprise for them."

The kitchen help were in their quarters near the stables. We went into the kitchen. We opened the iceboxes and we went into the storeroom and dumped the contents on the floor. We mixed sugar with salt and pepper with chocolate and nutmeg with cinnamon. We threw marmalade jars on the walls and the ceiling, we stuffed towels into the plumbing, and when we had done all the damage we could we opened all the water faucets all the way and let it run hot and cold. The kitchen was in the basement, the sewers were all blocked, and so it would fill up during the night, and everything would float in it. The Killer said we had to find the switch to cut the electricity.

As we came up out of the kitchen, I saw a flash of white gown and I ran after it. I was hot and covered with sweat, and I caught Reinhild by the hair. She screamed with fright. She never had allowed us any food between meals, no matter how hungry we were. I dragged her to the door of the kitchen and I said:

"I want some tea, Reinhild—and cake."

She said: "Now, Mademoiselle?"

I said: "Yes, now—Mademoiselle."

The kitchen was filling with water and I kicked her down the stairs and the Killer said:

"Let's drown her here. She can't get out, there are iron bars on the windows—or better still—when the water is high enough, we'll throw the switch and she'll be electrocuted."

Now she yammered and promised that she would not say a word to Papa, and this was the second time I had

her on her knees. She promised nothing would be said—
about Alain—about the night—about this, about anything
—nor would she breathe a word about the Killer, and she
was so abject, all her hauteur gone, that I let her go. Now,
like all of the help, she pressed herself against the wall
as she passed me, and avoided my eye. I embraced the
Killer and like my brother and Alain we said:

"Maintenant nous sommes des vrais durs. Maintenant
nous sommes des assassins."

The next morning around ten I went down into the
kitchen. They had already let the water out, the kitchen
beasts with their fat backsides were still kneeling and
mopping, the cooks were in furious haste to get things
ready for Papa's return.

Papa complained about the food during dinner. The
seasoning, he said, was awful and he said that he couldn't
stand German cooking any more and would get our chef
to come from France.

When Monsieur Bernard came, I almost felt sorry for
the help—he began a reign of terror. He screamed at them,
and when he disemboweled a fish or bird, he threw the
whole bloody mess on the wall. I went down there to watch
it and to see the help look stupefied like oxen hit on the
head, and run into each other and mumble bitterly with
their fat lips in their simple faces. I turned my back on
revenge quickly. The Killer asked me if I made Reinhild
bring me tea every afternoon.

I said, "No, because basically I am very kind and I can
never be bothered with revenge. I feel sorry for her—"

15. THE PROPOSAL

Alain and hugo were gone several months and there was no news from them; neither of them ever wrote. They had attended a school and gone through training, and then went to Indo-China, and whatever we knew about them was from reports that my father and Alain's received from the army.

Now everyone who was not in uniform was beginning to look like an American, especially the Germans. This was a remarkable transition, a mass change in personality. They all looked like the Americans in films. The same shirts, suits with overlong jackets, and lean jaws closely shaven. The Americans in civilian clothes were the only ones who didn't look like this. When they came with their cameras on vacation, they wore tropical-flowered shirts, and some of the men wore Tyrolean hats with feathers and shaving brushes on them. Among the French who arrived was one with a very American face and horn-rimmed glasses and the kind, impersonal expression of the well-bred college boy—he was the young Duke de la Rancheraye, very esthetic, very proper, long hands, long feet, a long body, athletic without looking like a wrestler or football player, very sensitive, exquisitely well brought up and mannered and quiet, and I knew that Mama would mention his name soon.

He had been sent on a cultural mission; it was his job to get the Germans to like impressionist painting, and French literature and history. He was here to bring about a better understanding. He was for all that was good, he was forever talking of ideals, and when he became too boring I said to myself: "Oh, what a pity that Alain and Hugo aren't here to argue with him." I did not argue, for all he said was right and proper.

He took me to French plays performed in a lovely small theater that had been built long ago, when French was the language of the small German courts. Because he had a long face and was always serious, I called him le Cheval Triste. Sad Horse read to me and he was very considerate. I was lonesome and I liked him to walk and talk with.

But the embarrassing moment came. One day in the park, with Hitler playing at my feet, my mother spoke to me. Her eyes were filled with an inner radiance new to me. I had never seen her like that. She always stood or sat like a somewhat bored plaster figure of Victory when she was next to my father, on the golf course, in the salons, in the reviewing stands, or at the bridge table. She turned her face to me, and with wide eyes she looked at me awhile —poor woman, who understood less of me than a cow does about Sunday—and then she started about Sad Horse. About his qualities, about his family, and then about his properties, which as the only child he would one day in-herit. The great house in the Rue de la Faisanderie, the

estate and horse-breeding farm in Deauville, the this and
the that, and in addition the other—and how wonderful
it would be if I, now, after all, would make the most
brilliant match of any girl in France and become the
Duchesse de la Rancheraye.

I listened to a description of Sad Horse—what charm,
what elegance, what manners, what sweetness. He does not
drink, take drugs, smoke, or chase women. He was the best
that France had to offer—although by this description he
wasn't French at all. And you can have him with your
little finger—Mama crooked her little finger and I was
sickened on poor Cyril's behalf. There is nothing more
disgusting than the calculation that goes into French arranged marriages and the corruption that they are infected
with from engagement to funeral. I said to my mother that
I preferred to be a whore rather than marry Cyril. She
managed to push out a cry of utter disgust, which was one
in a scale of sounds of despair, shrill and false. She leaned
away from me, and I made one of my declarations, namely
that there are far more whores in France among married
women who cheated their husbands, took their money, and
gave nothing in return than there were honest street-
walkers.

My mother closed her eyes and answered with sighs and
then a long profound silence. After this she regained her
mood of bliss, and contemplating the rings on her right
hand she continued: "I have given it a great deal of
thought. Cyril is the child of old people—his father begot
him after he was sixty, and his mother is not well—you
will not have to wait too long—and after you marry him—
and he adores you—you can lead him like a pony. It's all
very good, isn't it?"

"Yes, Mama, go on dreaming for me."

"Cyril is just the right age—now this doesn't happen to every girl, that a boy like that is offered on a platter—by his family in marriage. You like him physically?" My mother was now excessively gênée. When she had started to talk, she was very pale and now she blushed—and looked down. What hypocrisy, I thought.

"You have gone out in society and you know about life, and you have had everything, but in one respect you are still a little girl—" She kissed my brow, and I almost burst out laughing.

Hitler, who was also very delicate in personal matters, was hunching his back and trying to do his business in back of one of the numberless venerable linden trees that shielded the walks around Hohenlinden. My mother, more radiant than before, asked me to sit closer, and in this unbelievable moment started to give me a lecture on the intimate side of marriage. She looked out over the hedge of wild roses across the Moselle and she said in a shy voice: "My child, when one gives oneself to a man, to the man one loves—that is the most sacred and marvelous moment in a woman's life—and it is for life." She looked up into the foliage of the tree with an ecstatic expression. The wind was rustling in the linden leaves, and there was the smell of the wild roses.

Is it possible, I thought, to say all this and believe it? And what do I do now—play the sweet little idiot or tear down this lot of rot? I then thought this the moment to allow Mama to make herself completely ridiculous, and assumed the role of idiot. I asked her in as shy a voice as hers to tell me something about the things that happen when one marries. She avoided the subject and I became direct and asked very straight questions. She turned from me. I had hoped that she would say something like, well, you take off your clothes and then you do this or that. I was curious as to how she would explain it. I said impatiently: "Tell me."

There was a pause, Hitler was eating grass, which in Germany is taken as a sign of rain to come. Mama finally chose to be very old-fashioned French—and she said that at the proper time my husband would teach me, and that she was glad I inclined toward marriage at last. They always confuse bed with love and love with marriage and I tried to explain this to my mother only to find her bristling with shock. Sex and love are two entirely different things, I said to her. "But my child, precisely," she said. I said: "No, you mean love and marriage."

"Cyril," she said, ignoring my arguments, "is the ideal husband for you, sex, love, marriage, all in one. I think he should come and speak to Papa, and the sooner the better so we can make definite plans."

Now that would be gay. I saw in my mind how Cyril was removing his trousers—no, that always happens in cheap films. He would come in a magnificent robe de chambre from his apartment to mine, and all the servants would wait to hear the mattress going—no not that either, for it would take place in one of those awful hotels de luxe, on the honeymoon; in fact it would never come to pass at all, for I would never marry Cyril. Then I thought—while my mother went on into the department of trousseau, flowers, invitations, where and when, and what bishop, and servants and life with the gentry around the various estates, hunts, and balls—during this talk I imagined my father and mother making love—the General removing his trousers.

Once when I was afraid of him—when I was small—and wanted to overcome that, I sat on the toilet suffering from punishment and I imagined my father doing the same— and what had to be done before one left the cabinet, with paper and pulling the chain, and since then I have always imagined that when I was confronted with authority—I imagined them sitting on the toilet as I looked at them and it helped me to overcome any feeling of awe.

I did not hear the rest. Mama took my arm and we walked to the castle. I was a great deal with Sad Horse, and liked him, in spite of his apologies and his eternal doing good.

I had gotten out of most dinner parties and other functions by behaving badly and saying the things I thought. Now I was commanded to attend a dinner, and said dutifully: "Oui, mon Colonel, I shall be there." It was for Cyril and there was also a General, who was nice, and his wife. His name was Couvilier and he was intelligent, comfortable, and kind for a General.

His wife was vulgar. She always rode in the same manège as I, and once, just as I mounted my horse, she said: "Let's ride together."

I said: "Yes, sometime—Madame."

She said: "Where do you ride?"

So I said: "I love to ride alone in the Black Forest at night."

"Oh," she said, "does your father know about that?"

I said: "Yes, of course. He has forbidden it."

So she told my father about it and there was some difficulty which was finally settled when he agreed that I could ride, if the Killer went along at night—I mean when it was getting dark—to ride out in the late afternoon and come back in the darkness. We were not friends. She eventually divorced the General and married an industrialist. At this dinner she spoke of Chateaubriand, until I could no longer stand it. I said I was against romanticism, which was impuissant, like someone who makes love to his sister—untrue and sterile—and like velours and crêpe de Chine, draped over things that deserve much better—and that anyone with a mushy mind can get starry-eyed. When I get worked up I mount from ladder to ladder—up up up. Everyone looked at me with disapproval, and I expected that at any moment Papa would raise his arm and point and say "Go to your room." I had arrived at saying: "There is nothing more easy." She looked at me with the despicable tolerance of the middle-aged woman toward the young, and very condescendingly, and in her bourgeois voice and bad French she said: "What then, Mademoiselle, do you consider good writing?"

"Oh—Guillaume Apollinaire—Blaise Cendrars—and of course Baudelaire."

She said: "And Alfred de Musset—do you know his poetry?"

I said: "Allow me to quote him to you, Madame la Generale—

La lune sur un clocher

comme un point sur un i

signed Alfred de Musset, and written for housemaids." I said, "Excuse me," and got up and walked out into the garden. With unexpected courage Cyril got up and excused himself, and followed me into the garden. He was beside himself with admiration, and he said that he was completely of my opinion and he proposed—with the

moon sur un clocher—comme sur un i—and I said: "Don't
—I am very fond of you—but I could never love you." He
got on his knees, as in an Alfred de Musset poem—and I
can't stand men on their knees or anyone in a position of
dependence emotionally on another human being—or the
looks of love and handholding—all that revolts me.

I was sitting on the bench under the oldest of the linden
trees, poor Cyril on his knees before me, another who
wanted to attach himself to me, to enclose me. He tried
to embrace me and to kiss me, and words of love dribbled
from him. I listened until I couldn't stand it any more
and then I let him have it.

"I hate words like darling, baby, sweetheart, and phrases
like God bless you—and people who beg for love, or who
propose bed or who with sweet kisses and weak looks try
to advance their interests—it's like a disease oozing its
smeary infection. I can only be had by my own consent,
by wordless violence that is natural to me whenever and
wherever it takes place—and no matter how hurtful—or
how brutal."

He looked agonized—like a fish thrown on land, gulping for air. He had no answer. I said, "get up," the way you
say "sit down" to a dog.

When we came back from the park, my father, who like
my mother was also a hypocrite, did not slap me. He had
some champagne on ice. The other General and his wife
had departed. Papa said that he could not stand the vulgar
woman and could not understand how the General had
married her. I said, "Most probably he married her when
he was a Colonel"—and for that I didn't get a slap either.
Papa poured champagne. There were meaningful looks as

the glasses were raised—the Killer made faces at me from behind my father. My mother saw nothing as she was afloat in happiness. And then I went upstairs and Papa retired to his study for a heart-to-heart talk with his imagined future son-in-law—most probably giving him hints on how to handle me.

16. THE RETURN OF ALAIN

THE WHITE, LARGE BLOSSOMS of the tulip tree which
stood in front of my window had fallen to earth and they
lay on the road like shells along the sea. Beyond the road
was the carefully kept lawn and the yew hedge, black at
night, which framed the lawn as it rose up to the hill,
where the forest began. Above the treetops, which stabbed
like silver lances up into the sky, hung the moon.

It was one of many lonesome German nights, of absolute
quiet, once the trumpet had sounded retreat and the
steeples in the town below us had clanked away the time.
In these endless nights I sat on the balcony staring out
into this scene—every night since we had received the
news that my brother Hugo had fallen. On this night, the
gate was suddenly alight, and a moment after, with a blinding flash of headlights, a car raced into the enclosure
toward the house, coming to a stop under my window.
The Killer jumped from it and, as if it were a white dove,
he spun an envelope up into the air; it rose high above me,
and spiraled down to come to rest close to my feet.

I picked it up and the pain stopped, and I knew that the count of the dead that was in the reports from Indo-China was not for me. For here on the envelope was his handwriting. Alain was alive.

I opened it and read it as one eats when half dead of starvation. I read it without knowing what it said, but it stripped sorrow from me. Alain was not buried, he would be back. Miracle of love—he had never written a letter to anyone in his life.

The letter had been in my hands a few days when Alain's father received a report. Alain had been wounded. It was during the time when the commanding officer of one fort had ordered another officer to train guns on his position in case he was attacked. Alain was out at the head of a patrol trying to get through the lines. They were in a narrow passage when they were sighted by the enemy. Alain pressed himself close to a rock. A grenade missed him, but bit into the rock against which he had sought protection, and the explosion sheared away half his face, took the right ear and eye, and tore the right shoulder to pieces. He was out of the hospital, he was on his way to France.

When he arrived he went to his family's house in Paris. He wanted to see no one. He was there for a month. Then he phoned the Killer; he left a message for me to call him. Only his parents and the Killer and I knew about him.

I called him and I asked how he was, and I spoke as casually as I could. He believed that I did not know anything, and with a relieved voice he said that he was back for good, and felt a little tired and that for the time being he would stay in Paris and that he would like to see me. We made a rendezvous in a restaurant where he said we would

not be noticed and where we were not known—a place
called the Night and Day on the Champs Elysées.

I packed and took the train to Paris; and the next day
I dressed in three different outfits before finally deciding
on one in which I did not look like a nurse, like a jeune
fille, or too gay. I arrived, and on account of all that in-
decision about what to put on, I, who am always on time,
was fifteen minutes late and this was a terrible thing. I
entered the restaurant, which was deserted at this hour.
There was only one person sitting at a small table. I looked
around and since I did not see Alain, I sat down at the
first table, close to the door so that I would see him as he
came in. I checked my watch, and the man who was sitting
alone a few tables away got up and came forward and
stood in front of me and, suddenly, I said: "Alain!"

He said: "You see the worst side of me," and he moved
to the place on my right and said: "Let's sit here." On the
side where his eye and ear were, his profile was as before,
only the skin was patchy and gray and yellow, a straw-
color yellow, like the tobacco in English cigarettes. He
was very thin, his hands were thin and cold, and I asked
him if he wanted to stay or come home to his house or to
mine. He told me briefly what I already knew and he said
that in addition to the troubles that were evident in his face
he had attacks of malaria—and that to kill the pains of all
these afflictions he had to take a good many drugs, and that
he drank a great deal. There was nothing to do except to
put a bullet in his head, he said, and the purpose of meeting me was that, if there was any idea of obligation on my
part toward him, any bond between us, he wanted to tell
me to my face that it was over and that I was free.

I said the things one says and tried to console him.

He looked at me and shook his head—this half of his handsome face was hard as always. He said: "The army is finished with me. You are no longer for me. What shall I do? Run after women? Gamble? Drug myself? It's better to get it over with. Do you know what it is to look into the mirror when I awaken? To see this monstrous right side and, as if to mock me, the left side intact? To remind myself and everyone else that once I looked like a man? Shall I raise half a mustache—wear half a toupee? You haven't seen all of it—you didn't notice that I kept my hat on. I'm sorry—'a rotten heart but charm' they always said— 'unconquerable charm.' Well, no amount of charm can help me now. The pleasures are gone, and with every move there is another sensation of pain, and even to smile hurts me. Not amusing, any of this. Forgive me—I hate myself for exposing you to it, but I had to see you one last time— and so—I will never repeat it."

He asked for the check and while he paid it, now using a completely new set of gestures and motions, paying out with the one hand that was not injured, and stiffly getting up, he said in his bitter way that he had heard I had been seen with Cyril—he said it as casually as if it were a meaningless remark—he held the door open for me—he said he had heard that I might marry Cyril. I said that I was fond of him and he said that Cyril was a very nice boy, and that he wished me well. We got into the car and the chauffeur drove. I wanted to say: "Why do you torture me and yourself?" but his face stopped all conversation. We sat in awkward silence. He said that he might, if the doctors could make him tolerably free of pain, go into auto racing—now that there was nothing to lose but this miserable life. He said how lucky Hugo was, who had died in combat, face to face with the enemy—better than he who had tried to save himself. In this hopeless mood, he left me at the door of my house. I called him as soon as I thought he would be back at his home. The servant said he was still out, and he was out whenever I called the next days. I wrote to him—the letters were not answered.

17. FAREWELL TO YOUTH

IN THE MONTHS THAT FOLLOWED I heard that Alain had steadily improved and that he bought a racing car and was out practicing. I received an invitation to a soiree at a house in Neuilly. I found Alain there, cold as he had always been, and handsome. All that money, surgeons, skill, and courage to endure pain could accomplish had been done.

Now he had been drinking. His one sharklike eye shone, lit up emerald green, its pupil was contracted. His eye never left my face; it was as if he were sighting over a weapon at me.

Over the other eye he wore a blue velvet patch and again I thought how like a statue, how heroically elegant. As if it could not be otherwise. His hand was clamped about the glass he held, the lean fingers bloodless; he seemed to want to break the glass by pressure or to throw it. Cyril appeared and he behaved all evening as if we were engaged. He was sweet, and never anything but correct and kind—but always at my side. It was late, and became later, and we were the last people at the party. I had come in a taxi as Sad Horse's car was in the garage—Cyril's car was always in the garage being repaired or adjusted. Alain offered to take us home. He had all exits blocked, all excuses countermanded.

There were no taxis to be had—and it was late and the host wanted to go to bed. And there we were, in front of the heavy racing car. "Get in," Alain said. There were only two seats in the large car, but Sad Horse is very thin and obliging and always concerned for my comfort. He placed himself against the side, letting me sit in the center. Alain slammed the door and the engine roared. His mouth was a bitter gash, and I thought, God help us now.

He drove out toward the auto route. He said he knew that this was not the road home, but he wanted to show us what the machine could do, and how well he had learned to drive it with but one eye. The top was down. He switched on the heat that came from below and rolled up like a warm blanket. He came out of the tunnel and where it says to put out your lights, for the auto route is lit, he started racing, and the vehicle moved ahead effortlessly, soundlessly. As he drove to the end of the auto route, turned around, and raced back, it seemed as if we had merely driven through the Bois de Boulogne. We were at the exit at Vaucresson, a few miles from Paris, when he turned the car and drove into the forest that stands along the route.

He stopped in a place on a side road surrounded by trees, with no house, no light in sight—in the most terrible last-minute place in life. He pulled the hand brake, stopped the motor, and said: "Evidently we must come to some kind of agreement—we have to settle accounts for once and for all."

He took his hand off the brake and put it inside his coat pocket and from it brought a gun. "You are free I told you—" he began "—but not to marry that one at your side—you're not for him."

Cyril said: "Alain—please—!"

"If I want to, and I want to very much, I can finish all of us, now. Don't think I will hesitate—" He had the army automatic in his hand, and he raised it—he cocked it—and held it to my head.

I said to myself, now I have no defense, I cannot get out of the car—I am between the two. The one on my right cannot defend me, for even as he is, Alain is stronger than he, and twice as reckless. It is necessary then that I remain very quiet—that at no time will I answer, or provoke him, or make any remarks, or jokes even, for laughter may set him off as easily as anger. I must just sit still here—and if this is the end, then it is the end and there is nothing I can do about it. Alain looked at me all this time from the side, and on the other side I could hear Cyril breathing. He looked out into the forest. He held on to the side of the car like a bird afraid to fall out of its nest. He turned his nice clean and cool face toward us —and again I thought he would get us killed, for he said with awkward stammering: "Alain—you are not yourself. Please stop pointing this gun at this defenseless girl." Alain said some very rough words to him—told him to shut up, or he would be the first to get it.

Somehow Cyril got up courage enough in his cramped position to get at his cigarettes and a match, and he lit a cigarette, offered Alain and me a smoke, threw the match away, and assuming a casual and bored attitude he looked out into the dark forest.

"I'm doing you all a great service," said Alain, "especially you, Cyril." Alain, as if he had a swollen lip, slurring his words, said that I was a whore. He said: "However, don't worry—I have not been faithful either—I had every woman—white, yellow, black, and brown, nice women, whores like you, sick women—fat and thin—" He used the filthiest words, saying the same thing over and over again, accusing me of being unfaithful and while he did not want me—he would see to it that I was not marrying that one, on my right. He raged on in fury and screamed the obscene words and insults and all this time held the gun to my head. I don't know how long it would have lasted, except that Cyril suddenly got up and announced that he had had enough. He got out of the car, lit another cigarette, and walked away. We were alone.

I asked Alain where he had gotten the information that I was all that he said I was. He said he couldn't tell me. I said that obviously he had received letters from home—how else? He said that he had received one letter which he had read and thrown away; the others he had not even opened, but thrown into the fire.

He then said: "Swear to me that what was in them is not true—swear that to me, or I'll kill you—now—and myself as well."

I said: "If you believe that it is true then shoot—go on."

He said: "Oh God, oh my God," and he put the pistol back in his pocket. He called Cyril, who got back into the

car, and Alain drove back by way of Marnes la Coquette—
and then to Cyril's house in the Rue de la Faisanderie,
where he bid him good night as if nothing had happened.

On the drive back, I convinced myself that the author
of the letters Alain had received was Reinhild—who else
could have written them? It fit exactly. Her conferences
with Papa, her jealous hatred of my mother, her cold dislike of me, the desire to revenge herself on Alain—it all
pointed to her. I said nothing.

The city was quiet, the Champs Elysées deserted. Alain
stopped the car along the quays of the Seine and he said:

"Will you swear something?"

I said: "If you want me to swear that I was what is called
'true to you,' I certainly won't."

"No no no—" he said. "Only swear to me that from
now on you will avoid me—that you will never go to any
dinner, or party where I might be, for I love you so much,
and I am only death to you. Let me finish myself—and
don't get in my way— Oh good God, I almost did something terrible—you know at every second, and at every
word, I squeezed the trigger—why it didn't go off, why I
didn't kill you I don't know." Tears ran down his cheek.
Hard terrible Alain who never cried.

In the awkward and halting gestures conditioned by the
damage to his arm, he slowly brought a handkerchief out
of his pocket. And this to me was a heartbreaking flag of
truce. It was scented with lavender and it made me think
of Papa. But I no longer hated him. Like soft warm rain
a curtain descended on me. I thought of the little wild
pigs, the old toad whose pearly underside heaved when he
breathed, and I suddenly felt weak.

I put my arms around Alain. I said: "I will swear something to you." I kissed him on the side of all the hurt, on that part of his face which was like raw chicken flesh, and I said: "I will swear to you, Alain, that I will go wherever you go, that I will be at your side always, at every party and in every moment of danger, sorrow, and misery. And I swear I will never leave you, never."

THIS BOOK WAS SET IN

BASKERVILLE AND MASTERMAN TYPES,

PRINTED, AND BOUND BY

THE HADDON CRAFTSMEN.

DESIGN IS BY LARRY KAMP.